STAR TREK®

THE ORIGINAL SERIES

THE FOLDED WORLD

Jeff Mariotte

Based upon *Star Trek*
created by Gene Roddenberry

D1007404

POCKET BOOKS

New York   London   Toronto   Sydney   New Delhi

Pocket Books
A Division of Simon & Schuster, Inc.
1230 Avenue of the Americas
New York, NY 10020

This book is a work of fiction. Any references to historical events, real people, or real places are used fictitiously. Other names, characters, places, and events are products of the author's imagination, and any resemblance to actual events or places or persons, living or dead, is entirely coincidental.

First Pocket Books paperback edition May 2013

POCKET and colophon are registered trademarks of Simon & Schuster, Inc.

For information about special discounts for bulk purchases, please contact Simon & Schuster Special Sales at 1-866-506-1949 or business@simonandschuster.com.

The Simon & Schuster Speakers Bureau can bring authors to your live event. For more information or to book an event, contact the Simon & Schuster Speakers Bureau at 1-866-248-3049 or visit our website at www.simonspeakers.com.

Manufactured in the United States of America

10 9 8 7 6 5 4 3 2 1

ISBN 978-1-4767-0282-7
ISBN 978-1-4767-0284-1 (ebook)

The electrical green ribbons grew wider, their edges less distinct, until the entire field of view was a brilliant green. Blue-white lightning-like bolts shot across the screen, connecting with one another in an almost web-like construction, then faded out, leaving ghost-images burned onto the screen. That blue-white light spread until it was the dominant color; as soon as it was, it began to darken toward something more like traditional deep-space black, with pinpoints of light behind it. Then the process began again.

In the center of it all was the *McRaven*. Kirk still couldn't make out anything more than a smudge on the screen. "Enlarge again," he ordered. The captain settled into his seat, right elbow on the armrest, chin on his fist, as he watched the image seem to grow closer.

This time, he could barely make out the *McRaven*. She was a *Constitution*-class ship, like the *Enterprise*.

And she wasn't alone.

The *McRaven* was jammed into a conglomeration of spacegoing vessels, like part of a puzzle where the goal was to take apart the seemingly inextricably linked objects. All of them were clustered around another ship, one bigger than any Kirk had ever seen, as if it had attracted them with its own gravitational field.

"That's not possible," Kirk said.

"It is the *McRaven*," Spock assured him. "We have positively identified it."

"We're still picking up its distress beacon," Uhura said.

"But it looks like it's been there for decades."

"Indeed," Spock said.

"And it's only been days, if that."

"Correct."

This one's for Neil Armstrong and Eugene Cernan,
first and last. For now.

—*JM*

THE FOLDED WORLD

One

They emerged again on the third afternoon, when the scouts told them the giant had gone. Climbing the stairs, Aleshia peered into the frothy murk of low clouds. Giant's clouds. They would dissipate in a few hours, a day at the most.

Gillayne cleared the shelter's doorway ahead of her. She dropped to her knees on bare earth and a ragged cry tore from her throat. Aleshia stepped around her (Gillayne's narrow back, all hard wedges of shoulder blade and curled knuckles of spine, hitching with her liquid sobs) and saw what had elicited such an agonized wail.

The giant had walked right through town.

In his horrible, huge footprints lay the ruins of buildings—homes, barns, the children's school, all of it destroyed, flattened. Beams and timbers scattered and splintered, kindling for winter's fires, perhaps, but nothing more. Bricks and stones had been torn asunder and strewn about.

Aleshia's father cuffed the back of her head. "You're blocking the way, girl!" Startled, she took three stumbling steps and turned toward him. He glared at her, his thick lips curled in his usual disapproving sneer. Times like this, Aleshia was glad her mother was dead, so the woman who had brought her into this harsh life couldn't see what her husband had become. "There's no doubt cleaning to be done at home," he said. "I'll be around later."

This could only mean that he would go to Knott's tavern before coming home, drunk and even angrier. It still stood; somehow, giants never seemed to destroy Knott's. Simply strolling past it made Aleshia uneasy. She always felt that the people inside were eyeing her with malicious intent. It was even worse when her own father was among them, except that at least then she could count on being alone at home for a while. Those moments were the only times she felt truly comfortable there.

Always, though, he returned. Banging doors, upending furniture, shouting, threatening, and worse. Aleshia accepted her lot. What else was a girl to do? He beat her only rarely, and had never seriously injured her. She knew other girls in town who could not say the same.

She also knew some who were not beaten at all. Or so they claimed. She never altogether believed them.

The path home took her past one of the giant's footprints. Aleshia heard moans and cries as she neared it, and she hiked up her tattered skirts and ran to the side.

The sight made tears flood her eyes. The giant's

massive foot had collapsed one of the shelters. The earth was caved in, and most of the people hunkering inside were dead or injured. One man raised a scrawny arm toward Aleshia, beseeching her, but his legs were crushed, bone showing, blood soaking the dirt around him. There was nothing she could do by herself, so she turned away from his plaintive cries, seeking help.

Yignay, one of the village elders, walked toward her with his usual awkward gait; a childhood disease had left his spine twisted and his legs weak. She beckoned furiously, but he could not increase his pace. Finally, he came to a halt at the pit's edge.

"Do something!" Aleshia pleaded.

"Do what? We're all better off, anyhow. Fewer mouths there are to feed, fewer of us'll starve this winter."

"Yignay, you can't just—"

"I can't what? Ignore them? Watch me." He spat into the dirt and hurried away, as if those weren't his own townsfolk, his neighbors, suffering in that pit.

Aleshia looked down again. The people below called to her, begging. But she was just a barefoot girl, with no influence in the village and not enough strength to haul the injured from the pit. The stairs had collapsed, so ladders would have to be lowered. If she couldn't even get Yignay to help, she didn't know what she could do.

And her father expected her to have the house

cleaned up when he got home. If this was like the other times, it would be a mess. Furniture might be broken, and even if not, things would have tumbled from shelves and fallen from hooks. She tasted smoke on the air; people had run for the shelters so fast that they hadn't put out their fires, and now houses were burning. Hers was stone, small and sturdy and unlikely to burn. Still, she needed to be home before someone broke in, to steal whatever had not been lost to the giant's carelessness.

Aleshia ran again, this time not toward the pit but away from it. She told each person she encountered about the carnage, trying to send someone back who could offer aid to the wounded. In the time before she was born, her father had told her, people had cared about the troubles of others. That had changed, he said, as growing cities in the east had demanded ever more of the crops and livestock produced by the villagers. Feeding the cities had left the countryside hungry, and the hungrier they became, the less compassion they showed. Aleshia had been born hungry and had known no other life. She thought that people ought to be better than they were. In truth, however, little in her experience bore that out.

Several minutes later she had climbed the rocky slope to her house, gone inside, and barred the door. Beads of sweat ran down her cheeks, and her eyes stung from the smoke outside. The house yet stood, but it would need some work, as her father had guessed, and one window had cracked from the giant's passing. Father would replace that, or not, as he chose. If she caught him in a good mood, tomorrow or next week, she might suggest it.

Until then, she would hope to keep away from him, to escape his notice as much as she could. This was Aleshia's fate. Not a happy one, but she labored under no illusion that life was meant to be happy. She was hungry but not starving, and as healthy as anyone could expect. She had walls to keep out the cold and a roof to block the rain. She had a father to protect her against threats from other folk, though she sometimes wondered if those threats could prove more hurtful than his own attacks.

Happiness? That was for dreams, nothing more. Even then, she knew it was illusion. When she was happy in a dream, she wept upon waking, because she knew that it was imaginary and fleeting. It would never last. Was this really all there was in life, all she had to look forward to? Growing old amid hunger and heartache, living in fear of tomorrow and the day after that? Somewhere, she had to believe, things were better. Not here, not for her . . . but perhaps there was a way to find such a place, if it existed.

Those were foolish thoughts, however, that had nothing to do with her life or her future. She was locked in place, and she would stay there until she died, until a giant strolled through town and crushed her under his heel. And that, she thought, might be more merciful than more years of labor for her father and then for some other man, a husband. Knowing the road ahead, Aleshia sat on the stone floor, amid broken crockery and shattered glass, buried her face in her skirts, and cried.

And when she was finished crying, she got to work.

Two

"Captain's log, Stardate— No, wait, never mind. Abort recording." James T. Kirk rose from his captain's chair and walked to the viewscreen at the front of the bridge, as if he could stand there and see home.

"Is everything all right, Captain?" Nyota Uhura asked.

"Yes," he said, aware that he sounded as distracted as he felt. "Yes, Lieutenant. Everything is fine, thank you. It's just . . . I had forgotten the date."

"Stardate is—"

"No, I mean the *real* date. Back home."

"The sixth of August," Lieutenant Sulu said from his position at the helm.

"Yes," Kirk said again. "That's right."

The captain peered into the darkness of deep space. The crew of the *Enterprise* would understand the date's significance if he explained it. But they had a starship to operate, and the story would take too long to tell properly. It had started during his thirteenth year, when he and eight others witnessed the massacre of four thousand colonists on the planet called Tarsus IV.

Following that trauma, his parents had decided that he'd be better off on Earth for a while. His parents' Starfleet careers didn't allow them to remain planetside for long, but young Jim Kirk was dropped off at his uncle Frank's farm in Idaho, a lush, green spread that shouldered up against the Rocky Mountains. He stayed for just over a month, and the period meant to be recuperative turned out to also be transformative.

While he was there, he accompanied Uncle Frank and one of Uncle Frank's best friends, a rancher named Ned Devore, on a cattle drive. Ned had several hundred head of cattle that needed to be moved out of a high-elevation summer pasture to their winter range. Kirk found himself on horseback, working alongside a dozen men, putting in long days in the saddle and nights around a campfire, listening to lies and stories, laughing, eating everything put before him and longing for more. He slept bundled in a bedroll beneath stars that looked, to his then-untrained eye, just like the ones he saw now through the viewscreen, and he woke on chilly mornings to the smells of coffee and bacon and livestock. He knew, even at that age, that he was tasting a vanishing way of life, connected by invisible threads to the generations who had come before.

His horse, a big, black stallion named Champ, might have seemed fearsome had he not been so gentle. Boy and mount developed a fierce bond during their two weeks together, a happenstance he had not expected but found that he enjoyed. The whole adventure had instilled in him a love of the outdoors, particularly in the North American West, that had stayed with him ever since. It had also deepened his connection with Uncle Frank, and helped him heal from the tragedy on Tarsus IV.

His last day with Uncle Frank, during which they were both recovering from the days on horseback, reliving parts of the cattle drive, and generally enjoying one another's company, had been the sixth day of August. Kirk remembered the date, because the next day had been Uncle Frank's birthday. He also remembered it because a year later, to the day, Uncle Frank had been struck by a massive heart attack while splitting firewood in his side yard. He had, most likely, died instantly.

Small comfort, that.

Most years since then, unless circumstances had not allowed, Kirk thought about his uncle Frank on that date; remembered especially those magical days and nights of the cattle drive, riding through fragrant mountain meadows and clear, icy streams, hearing the thunder of hooves and the calls of night birds and the raucous laughter of men who worked hard and loved life. He recalled the way Uncle Frank had smelled, of sweat and horse and wood smoke, the way his laugh boomed so loud it seemed to echo from the canyon walls, the way he called Kirk "Jimmy-boy," with the emphasis on the *Jim*.

Service on a starship had much in common with that experience, he thought. The ship's crew comprised both men and women, not just men, but they were as dedicated to their task as those long-ago cowboys had been. Their camaraderie, tested by blood and fire, was strong. They worked toward goals that mattered.

Kirk turned away from the viewscreen and swept his gaze across the bridge, taking in Sulu and Uhura and Chekov and Spock, seated as usual with his back to the others, the only one not watching to see if their captain had lost his mind. "Sorry," Kirk said. "I'm back."

"Back from where, Captain?" The turbolift door whooshed closed behind the newcomer. He was Levi Michael Gonzales, a Federation diplomat. He was a lean man, tall and stoop-shouldered, with a craggy face and a nose that jutted from it like the prow of a sailing ship. His hair was long, hanging to his mid-back, and mostly silver. To Kirk, the odor that always wafted around him smelled slightly rancid, like a pork chop left too long in the sun.

"A figure of speech, Mister Gonzales," Kirk said. "I was lost in thought for a moment, that's all."

"Happens to the best of us," Gonzales said, as if Kirk were somehow not in that exalted rank with the diplomat and might appreciate the assurance of his betters.

"Is there something I can help you with, Mister Gonzales?"

"Minister Chan'ya would like to know what our progress toward Ixtolde is."

You can tell Minister Chan'ya to just subtract six hours from the last time she asked, Kirk thought. But Gonzales was a Federation official and Chan'ya an Ixtoldan government representative, and neither category of people, in his experience, was famous for their sense of humor. "I believe we're still on course," Kirk said. "Mister Chekov?"

The young ensign consulted his screen for only an instant. "Eight days, four hours, and thirteen minutes until we reach Ixtoldan orbit," Chekov said. His Russian accent and clipped manner of speaking somehow lent his pronouncement extra weight.

"There you go," Kirk said. "Is there anything else?"

Gonzales let out the briefest of sighs. "I understand that she can seem like a handful, Captain," he said softly. "But she is important in the Ixtoldan hierarchy, and Federation membership is important to the whole planet. You won't be burdened with her for too much longer, I promise."

"It's no burden at all, Mister Gonzales." Not strictly true, but Kirk was no stranger to diplomacy himself.

"Thank you for saying so, Captain Kirk. And a little professional advice? When you tell a lie, try to tame that twinkle in your eyes. It's your tell. I doubt that Chan'ya has enough experience with humans to catch it, but it's obvious to me."

The diplomat returned to the turbolift without waiting for a response. Once the door had closed behind him, Uhura said, "I guess he told you!" and let out the laugh she had been holding in. Kirk, Sulu, and Chekov joined in.

Spock looked on, his expression typically impassive. "You might recall my mentioning that as well, Captain," he said. "While I claim no expertise in lying, I share the gentleman's opinion that if it is something one has reason to do, it had best be done as well as possible. The point is not to be found out, is it not?"

"That is indeed the point, Mister Spock," Kirk said. "I will take your advice, and Mister Gonzales's, under serious advisement." He caught Uhura's gaze as he spoke, and held it. Then he asked, "Any twinkle?"

"Only the faintest, Captain," Uhura replied. "I think you've nearly got it."

". . . out there, the universe is vast, and it doesn't care about you." Petty Officer First Class Miranda Tikolo spoke fast, and she talked with her hands, waving them both in different directions, as if to indicate where the universe might be in relation to their table in the crew mess. "It doesn't care whether you live or die. Some of those who inhabit it do, certainly—some would kill you as soon as look at you, and take great joy in doing it." She shuddered, and Paul O'Meara knew she was thinking of the Romulans. "But I have to think there are some who are friendly, and wise, and have something to offer besides death and destruction, don't I? Or else what am I doing here? Why are you looking at me like that?"

Because you're absolutely stunning, O'Meara thought. "I only asked you if you wanted to work out with me later," he said.

"Oh, right," she said. "I'm sorry, I can't. I've got an appointment with . . . somebody else."

"Stanley."

She let out a little sigh. "Yes, Stanley."

"You can say his name, you know. It's okay."

"I know," Tikolo said. "Only it's—I don't know. Awkward. I'm sorry."

"Don't be." He tried to follow the threads of their conversation. He had been eating his meal without tasting it, because his senses had been focused on her: the delicious way she smelled, like the first peach of summer, the way the light played on her lustrous black hair and caught the highlights of her dark eyes, the way her lips, so perfectly shaped, closed over her fork when she took a bite. He was admiring the way her short red dress hugged her figure when she looked up from her food and caught him staring. The idea of spending some time in the gym with her sprang to mind, and he went with it. Somehow she had used that invitation to expound a philosophical treatise on the necessity of exercise, because, as she explained, the universe was either uncaring or downright hostile, so a person had to keep her body in excellent physical condition, to be ready to defend herself against any danger at any moment.

O'Meara understood, or thought he did, the mental paths she had taken. She rarely talked about her experiences on and off Earth Outpost 4 when the Romulans attacked, but he could see the fallout in the haunted look in her eyes, the way she flinched at loud noises, even the way it sometimes took her longer to laugh than it did other people. Miranda had been thoroughly vetted and cleared for duty, and he had no worries about her psychological state. That did not mean, however, that she was free of those memories, or would ever be.

Mostly, when he looked at her, he saw the most beautiful woman he had ever met, and more and more often he found himself wondering if what he felt was love or just something very much like it.

And then there was Stanley Vandella. O'Meara saw the way Vandella stared at her, and it was like watching his own reflection in a mirror. Vandella felt the same way he did, and if Tikolo had a preference between them, she didn't let on.

That couldn't last much longer. O'Meara tried to pretend it didn't matter to him, that he was fine with any decision, or the lack thereof. But as his feelings deepened—and already his heart seemed to stop every time he got a glimpse of her in the corridor, much less touched her velvet skin or earned a smile or a kiss—he knew he wouldn't be able to stand it much longer. At some point, she would have to choose. She could pick him or she could pick Stanley or she could even say that she would continue on with both of them, but she would have to definitively say where her heart was.

Three

Kirk sat at the desk in his quarters, answering communications and checking over status reports from crew members and Starfleet headquarters back on Earth. Running a starship sometimes meant making snap life-and-death decisions or facing down existential threats, but more often than not it was a matter of dealing with the forms, reports, and queries common to bureaucracies across the known universe. Right now, he would willingly have swapped all the busywork for a single megalomaniac determined to rule his quadrant of space.

So when he heard the door buzzer, Kirk was delighted at the interruption. "Come," he said, knowing that the number of people who would have interrupted him was a small handful.

The door opened and Doctor Leonard McCoy walked in, his expressive brow furrowed. He was carrying a bottle and two shot glasses. Without a word, he poured out two fingers. The doctor raised his glass and offered, "Uncle Frank."

Kirk raised his own glass and drank. The captain suppressed a cough. "Red-eye whiskey, Bones?"

"I remember you telling me it was his favorite. Not one of mine." McCoy took the visitor's chair and poured them both another shot. He sat looking down, swirling the whiskey along the sides of the glass.

"Spit it out, Doctor."

"I just had a visit from Petty Officer Tikolo," McCoy said.

"How's she doing?"

"Without jeopardizing patient confidentiality, I can say that she's better than she has a right to be."

"As the captain of this ship, I have a right to know about crew—" Kirk began, but McCoy cut him off.

"I know, Jim. You're the captain. I'm the chief medical officer. That means I have to balance priorities. I'm tryin' to thread a needle, here."

Kirk settled back in his chair. "Thread away, Bones. Tell me what you can."

McCoy leaned casually on his right armrest. "You're aware of her situation."

"Of course." About a year ago, a Romulan bird-of-prey had violated the Neutral Zone, established after the Earth-Romulan War, and had attacked a series of Federation outposts established to keep an eye on the zone. The *Enterprise* had destroyed the Romulan ship—learning, in the process, that the Romulans had developed cloaking technology that, despite some flaws, was more effective than anything in Starfleet's bag of tricks—but not before the Romulans had vaporized several of the outposts.

Miranda Tikolo had been assigned to Outpost 4 for just over a year when the attacks came. A skilled pilot, she had been flying a cargo run between Outposts 3 and 4 when the Romulans struck. Witnessing the destruction of the outpost and her crewmates—and, via her instruments, the pitched battle between the *Enterprise* and the Romulans—she had shut off all the shuttle's systems and drifted in space, hoping not to be noticed. Once the battle was over, she had hailed the *Enterprise*. They had picked her up, astonished to learn that there was even a single survivor from Outpost 4.

Tikolo had been appreciative, and had enjoyed her time on board the starship. When Starfleet's medical personnel cleared her for duty, she requested assignment to the *Enterprise*, which the captain had gladly approved. She had been part of the security detail for seven months now, and Kirk was happy with her performance.

"Given what she went through—all those hours in the dark, alone, floatin' in space, watchin' her crewmates killed right in front of her—it's no surprise that she continues to have some psychological scarring. Those scars don't go away."

"Bones, are you saying there's a problem?"

"I wouldn't call it that, exactly. She's been havin' nightmares. I think they were prompted by that Ixtoldan battle cruiser accompanying us on this trip. She's only had a glimpse of it, and while it doesn't look

much like a Romulan bird-of-prey, I expect she's con-
flated the two in her mind."

"She can't expect to serve on a Starfleet vessel and
never encounter an alien ship," Kirk said.

"I'm sure she doesn't. And I should add that I don't
believe she's a danger to herself or anyone else. It's just
that the bad dreams bothered her enough that she felt
it necessary to tell me about them. It's classic survivor's guilt, Jim. I can say that I understand, but—"

All at once the captain understood what his friend
was asking. "Doctor McCoy, you are overstepping—"

"No, I'm not. The crew knows about Tarsus IV.
Tikolo needs someone she looks up to. She needs an
Uncle Frank."

Finally Kirk said, "Okay, Bones. As soon as I get a
chance—"

The boson's whistle announced a call from the
bridge, and Uhura's voice followed. *"Captain,"* she said.
"We're receiving a distress hail from the U.S.S. McRaven."

The *McRaven* was a Starfleet ship that had left Earth
a few days before the *Enterprise,* her mission so classified that even Kirk didn't know what it was. Because
she was following essentially the same course as the
Enterprise, he assumed the mission had something to
do with their own: ferrying Minister Chan'ya and her
retinue to Ixtolde, along with the Federation delegation.
Ixtolde was an impoverished planet, the sole inhabited
world in its solar system. But its populace had acquired
the capability for interstellar travel, and had applied

for Federation membership. Everybody wanted it to happen. Trade helped make planets prosperous, and Ixtolde had untapped mineral resources to which others wanted access. The idea was that the *Enterprise* and the *Ton'bey*, the Ixtoldan battle cruiser, would arrive together in Ixtoldan space. Other Ixtoldan ships would meet them there, and the combined delegations would be shuttled to the planet's surface for a grand entrance.

The diplomats were negotiating with Chan'ya en route, and once they reached Ixtolde they would embark on a fact-finding tour of the world, to ascertain that it met the Federation's membership requirements. Kirk wasn't sure how the *McRaven* fit in, but he was convinced it had a role to play.

"How far behind are we?" Kirk asked.

"*The* McRaven *appears to be immobilized*," Uhura reported. "*Although it has been four days ahead of us, at our current speed we're only about a day behind.*"

"Do we know the nature of their emergency?"

"*No, sir. I've been trying to raise them, without success. We're just getting the automated distress call.*"

Kirk met McCoy's gaze. One of the doctor's eyebrows arched slightly. The captain knew well what that meant. He was curious, too. "Inform the Ixtoldan ship. Intercept course. Warp six," he said. "I'm on my way."

By the time he and McCoy reached the bridge, Gonzales and a couple of the other diplomats, Perkins and Rinaldo, were already there. So were Minister

Chan'ya and three additional members of her party. Ixtoldans were generally humanoid in appearance, but with skin that appeared at most times to have been dusted with gold. The colors of the crystalline matter creating that impression could change, under intense emotional stimulus, turning a glowering purple when an Ixtoldan was angry and a deep sea green, according to reports, when sexually aroused. Chan'ya's had been a pale gold as long as Kirk had known her, although he noticed as he stepped off the turbolift that it was slightly more pronounced than usual.

The minister was shorter than Kirk and broader through the shoulders, with thick arms and legs and a sturdy torso. She wore a floor-length dress that appeared to be composed of a series of ribbons partially interwoven and wrapped tightly around her, in various shades of red and yellow. Her hair was pulled back off her face and braided into shoulder-length coils, each braid comprising white, gold, and silver strands. Kirk had not spent a lot of time with her, but he knew her well enough to realize that although her even-featured, seemingly guileless face appeared to betray an utter lack of sophistication, that was an illusion. She was not to be underestimated.

The other two Ixtoldans were even taller than Gonzales, towering over their minister, and both thin as rails. This told Kirk that Ixtoldans were a physically diverse people, similar in coloration but not necessarily in size and build.

Chan'ya greeted Kirk with a challenge. "Are we to understand, Captain, that our arrival at Ixtolde is to be delayed?" She spoke in a low, throaty mumble, hard to hear, but with each word distinctly pronounced. Her English was almost without accent.

"I'm not sure yet," Kirk replied. "A Federation starship is in some sort of trouble. We've increased our speed, and since the *McRaven* was following what appears to be the same course that we are, we are not necessarily losing any time. But it depends on what we find when we reach her."

"Still, we must register a protest. Our schedule is inviolate."

"Surely you understand, Captain Kirk," Gonzales added. "We've been invited as guests to their planet, and the schedule was established well before we left."

"I do understand," Kirk said. Turning to the Ixtoldan, he said, "I'm sorry, Minister Chan'ya. This can't be helped. I know you're not suggesting that we ignore a distress call."

"We suppose that we cannot," Chan'ya said with resignation. "But we expect that the utmost haste will be expended in addressing the situation, whatever it might be."

"Believe me," Kirk said, "if the *McRaven*'s in trouble and there's something we can do to help, we won't waste any time." He glanced toward Gonzales. "I'd expect Federation personnel to understand *that*."

"Oh, of course," Gonzales said quickly. "Obviously,

the safety of the ship and crew are the first priority. All I'm saying is, let's keep our mission schedule in mind."

Kirk held his tongue. What he wanted to say would not have been at all diplomatic. Finally, he trusted himself to speak again. "Of course."

"Very well, then."

Chan'ya gave Kirk a look that he couldn't quite read. She might have been wishing some painful and long-lasting death for him, or she could simply have been checking the color of his eyes. Or searching for that damn twinkle. During the time she'd been on the ship, he'd had a hard time reading her moods or her body language. But her skin turned slightly rosy, almost like a blush, and she pressed her hands against her sides and rushed from the bridge. Her retinue followed just as swiftly. None of them had uttered a word, but as the turbolift doors closed, the tallest of them shot Kirk an angry glare. His skin darkened, his lips drew back to expose a row of sharp yellow teeth, and his nostrils flared.

There was no mistaking the meaning of that.

Four

Doctor McCoy escorted the Federation delegation off the bridge as the captain took his seat, for the moment content to watch his crew do what they did so well. They were seasoned professionals and they worked with the crisp efficiency that he enjoyed, the way that some people did a well-choreographed ballet.

After a few minutes he heard his first officer punching buttons. "Is everything okay, Mister Spock?" he asked.

"We appear to be having an instrument malfunction, Captain. I am unable to determine the cause."

"It's here too, Captain," Chekov said anxiously. "Either we're spinning in circles, or my instruments are completely haywire."

Kirk stood up, leaning forward to check Chekov's display panel. "Mister Sulu?" he asked.

"Aye, Captain," Sulu reported. "I believe our systems are still functional at this point, and we remain on a steady course. But you wouldn't know it from the readings I'm getting."

"Captain?" Uhura said.

"Yes?"

"When you asked me about the *McRaven*'s course, she was following the same course that we had observed, until about this point. Then she diverted, rather markedly."

"So you're thinking there's something about this location that interferes with a ship's instrumentation. And when the *McRaven* went off course, it ran into trouble."

"It's a theory, sir."

"One with which I concur, Captain," Spock said. He was bent over his console, trying to rein in his instruments. From what Kirk could tell, without notable success.

"*Engineering to bridge!*" The voice over the intercom belonged to Chief Engineer Montgomery Scott. "*Captain! I dinna know what's goin' on with the instruments here, but I'm losin' all control of the engines!*"

"Full stop," Kirk instructed.

"Full stop," Sulu repeated, already moving to implement the command.

"*Far as I can tell, Captain, we're stopped,*" Scotty said a moment later. "*It's hard t' know for certain.*"

Kirk rose from his chair and went to the viewscreen. Even in the depths of space, with all the starship's environmental controls and artificial gravity fully functional, there was a faint but constant sensation of motion. He didn't sense it now. "I believe we are," he said. "Now, reverse thrusters. Slow and steady. Let's back out to where things started going haywire."

The slightest lurch indicated that the *Enterprise* was once again in motion. Most people—those not as attuned to the rhythms of the vessel as he was—would not have felt it. Even Kirk couldn't have said definitively whether they were moving forward or back. He trusted his crew, though, and both Scotty and Sulu had said they were *losing* control, not that control had already been lost. Given that, he believed a controlled reverse was achievable, and if Spock was right about the source of the instrument trouble, then getting out of range of whatever had caused it might set things straight.

He returned to his chair, but he didn't have to wait long for the answer. "Instruments normal," Sulu said after a few minutes.

"Here too, Captain," Uhura added.

Kirk touched his intercom controls. "Kirk to engineering," he said. "What about you, Mister Scott? Back to normal?"

"*Aye, Captain, it seems so,*" Scotty said.

"We're going to stay put and try to figure out what's going on," Kirk said. "We'll probe the vicinity from here and see what we find." He rose from the chair again. "Call me when you learn something," he added. "I've got to pay someone a visit."

He found Miranda Tikolo in her shared quarters. When she called out for him to enter, her voice sounded far away. He went in and she was sitting on the edge of her bed, her eyes vacant. After he stood there a moment, she focused on him.

"Captain," she said. "This is . . . a surprise."

"I just wanted to drop in, see how you're doing," he said.

She smiled. He had heard that the petty officer was the subject of possible romantic interest from more than one member of the ship's crew, and seeing the way her smile lit the room, he understood why. "Okay," she said. Her tone was sincere, in his judgment. And a person didn't become a starship captain without plenty of experience reading other people. "Captain, I want to thank you again for making me part of your crew."

"No thanks necessary," he said. "You earned that."

"Still, I—"

"Miranda," he interrupted. "I know you've been talking with Doctor McCoy, and that's good. What you've been through isn't easy, but it's a load you don't have to carry alone. I want you to understand that you can talk to Bones, you can talk to me—this ship is full of sympathetic ears."

"Thank you, sir. I understand."

He wasn't sure he was making himself clear. Tikolo's verbal responses seemed to indicate that he was getting through, but her facial expression hadn't changed. She looked like someone pretending to appreciate her gifts at a party, where the givers were watching her open every package. "There will be plenty of times when others are counting on you. You just need to know—"

She started to reply, but the intercom system cut her off. "*Bridge to Captain Kirk,*" Uhura said.

He went to the wall unit and activated it. "Kirk here."

"*Captain, I think we've found something.*"

"What is it?"

Instead of Uhura's voice, he heard the first officer's. "*You need to see this for yourself, Captain,*" Spock answered. "*It is most unusual.*"

Five

When Kirk stepped onto the bridge, everybody was staring at the viewscreen. It only took him an instant to understand why.

"The anomaly you see, Captain," Spock explained, "is what we believe to be the cause of our instrument malfunction."

"We were heading straight for it, Captain," Sulu said. "See that speck near the center? That's the *McRaven*."

"Enlarge," Kirk said.

"Aye, sir." Sulu touched a button and the image on the screen was magnified. It looked like nothing Kirk had ever seen. What should have been the black emptiness of deep space was instead shot through with jagged strands of green light that were constantly shifting. It reminded Kirk of nothing so much as electricity arcing from one point to another. The stars on the far side of the strange energy field behaved oddly, too—instead of giving off their usual brittle glow, they seemed to pulse, appearing to grow and shrink, and at the same time becoming more and less distinct.

As the captain watched, the scene changed. The electrical green ribbons grew wider, their edges less distinct, until the entire field of view was a brilliant green. Blue-white lightning-like bolts shot across the screen, connecting with one another in an almost web-like construction, then faded out, leaving ghost-images burned onto the screen. That blue-white light spread until it was the dominant color; as soon as it was, it began to darken toward something more like traditional deep-space black, with pinpoints of light behind it. Then the process began again.

In the center of it all was the *McRaven*. Kirk still couldn't make out anything more than a smudge on the screen. "Enlarge again," he ordered. The captain settled into his seat, right elbow on the armrest, chin on his fist, as he watched the image seem to grow closer.

This time, he could barely make out the *McRaven*. She was a *Constitution*-class ship, like the *Enterprise*.

And she wasn't alone.

The *McRaven* was jammed into a conglomeration of spacegoing vessels, like part of a puzzle where the goal was to take apart the seemingly inextricably linked objects. All of them were clustered around another ship, one bigger than any Kirk had ever seen, as if it had attracted them with its own gravitational field.

"That's not possible," Kirk said.

"It is the *McRaven*," Spock assured him. "We have positively identified it."

"We're still picking up its distress beacon," Uhura said.

"But it looks like it's been there for decades."

"Indeed," Spock said.

"And it's only been days, if that."

"Correct."

Kirk swiveled to look at Spock. The Vulcan sat at his station with a slightly annoyed expression. Spock didn't like not being able to explain something, but it was clear that this fell into the category of things he had not figured out. *Yet*, Kirk knew. *Give him time.*

"Any sign of life?" Kirk asked.

"We've been scanning, sir," Spock reported. "No carbon-based life that we can detect from here. And none of the systems on any of those ships appear to be functioning. It is possible that our distance, combined with the unknown qualities of the anomalous region, is skewing our readings, though."

"So we won't really know anything until we get closer. And we can't get closer."

"It would be inadvisable," Spock stated.

"It may be," Kirk said. "But that's a Starfleet ship out there. Unless we know beyond any doubt that there are no living beings on board, we're going to act as though there are. This has just become a rescue mission. I want every effort put toward figuring out what that anomalous region is, and how we can get to the *McRaven*." He paused a moment, knowing that his crew would understand the unspoken coda. Then he said it anyway, because sometimes it was better to make sure everybody heard the same thing in the captain's own voice. "And I want it done fast. Lives are on the line, and every minute counts."

Ixtoldan air was slightly more oxygen-rich than that found on Earth, or on board the *Enterprise*. In their own quarters, the Ixtoldans could adjust the mix, but in public spaces, like the ship's conference room, their breathing was loud and ragged as they drew in deep, rattling breaths. The conference table was packed with Chan'ya and her retinue, the Federation delegation, and Kirk, Spock, and McCoy.

"How long will it take?" Gonzales asked. Chan'ya sat at a side of the three-sided table, opposite Kirk. Her fellow Ixtoldans flanked her on her right, and the Federation diplomats on her left, with Gonzales immediately beside her. The symbolism of it disturbed Kirk; he understood the nature of the Federation mission, but believed that the organization's interests were in line with Starfleet's, and that should have been expressed in the seating arrangement.

"Since we don't yet know the nature of the situation," Kirk said, "I can't answer that."

"An estimate, surely?" Chan'ya asked. "We have been patient thus far."

Kirk didn't have to spend much time in a room full of diplomats to feel his own patience slipping away. "My estimate, Minister," he said, "is that it'll take as long as it takes. We will not abandon a Starfleet vessel in trouble."

McCoy put his hands down on the table, probably more forcefully than he had intended. "You people have got to understand," he declared. "Lives are at stake!"

"Everybody is aware of that, Doctor McCoy," Gonzales said. His tone was somewhere between ingratiating and patronizing, but closer to the latter.

"Then stop tryin' to pressure the captain and worry about those folks on the *McRaven*."

"My reason for asking you to join us here," Kirk said quickly, hoping to calm Bones before he escalated the disagreement into an interplanetary incident, "was to let you know, at once, what we're up against. I wanted you to hear it from me. We're still studying the anomaly, and trying to determine the safest way to proceed. There's an unexplained field. Within that field are an assortment of starships, only one of which we can identify at this point, clustered around another vessel, which is truly massive. So far, we haven't detected any definitive life signs, but we have picked up weak electrical impulses that seem to be centered aboard the big ship. We have no explanation yet for those."

He paused to let all that sink in, then added, "As we learn more, I'll keep you all informed. Just know that we are trying to determine with certainty whether the *McRaven* crew is still alive."

"And *our* mission must take second place?" Chan'ya asked, her flesh edging past rose.

"For now, yes. I'm sorry, but that's where things stand. If it's absolutely imperative that you reach Ixtolde on the original schedule, we could beam you over to your own ship, Minister. I'm sure the *Ton'bey* would be able to get you there on time."

"But Captain Kirk," the diplomat named Perkins said. "That would defeat the entire purpose. The idea was to have the minister and her people arrive on a Starfleet vessel, thereby demonstrating peaceful cooperation between the Federation and the Ixtoldans."

"I'm afraid it's one or the other, Mister Perkins. Either the schedule is kept, *or* they arrive on the *Enterprise*. It's not going to be both."

"I'm certain that we all understand what's at stake, Captain," Rinaldo said. Her eyes narrowed, and parallel ridges formed between them. "And we appreciate your concern for the *McRaven*. That said, you must understand that we'll have to discuss your attitude with your superiors at Starfleet."

"You are certainly free to do so," Kirk added calmly.

This time, McCoy slammed the table with intent. "Remind them that you're Federation officials and you're dismissing the value of lives. That's something I believe even civilian officials swear to place above all else."

"You must forgive Doctor McCoy, Minister," Kirk said. "As a doctor, he has a particular obligation to help those in need. At any rate, I'm going to put these conversations in the ship's log and in my official report," he added, fully aware that no matter how right McCoy was, there was no way a bureaucrat could admit it. "And I'm sure none of you were suggesting that we forgo our rescue mission."

"In a pig's eye," McCoy muttered.

"That, I must admit, is an expression I have never understood," Spock said.

"I'll explain it to you sometime when I'm not bitin' mad," McCoy offered.

"Minister Chan'ya, Mister Gonzales, I think we're finished here. We are all on the same page, correct?" Kirk said.

Gonzales met the minister's gaze for a long moment. Whatever passed between them, Kirk couldn't make out, but it seemed to be good enough for them. "Yes, Captain," Gonzales said. "Carry on with your rescue mission. The minister holds every hope for its successful conclusion."

"I appreciate that," Kirk said. He didn't necessarily believe it. But he did appreciate the sentiment being expressed.

Because either way, he was going to get to the *McRaven*.

All he had to do was figure out how.

Six

For a long time after joining the *Enterprise* crew, Miranda Tikolo had looked forward to meals in the crew mess, because they meant being surrounded by her peers. People talked and laughed, debated and pontificated, but there was generally a good-natured sociability that she enjoyed. The detachment assigned to Earth Outpost 4 had been a small one, and when that duty station had come to its tragic end, she had been entirely alone, on a tiny shuttlecraft, watching a Romulan bird-of-prey vaporize everyone. Since then, she had often sought out the comfort of crowds. She needed a certain amount of alone time—every human being did, she believed, and probably other races did as well—but she never wanted it to last very long, and she always felt somewhat ill at ease when she couldn't see other people.

Lately, though, both Paul O'Meara and Stanley Vandella had started putting pressure on her to choose one of them. She didn't want to do that, or even to limit herself to just those two men. Both were decent and kind, capable lovers if not spectacular, easy enough to look at. But neither one made her heart race and her breath catch, not the way Eric Rockwell had, back on Outpost 4. She didn't know if that was because something had broken inside her, or if it had to do with them. But she wasn't ready to give up hoping that she could have it again someday, and Vandella and O'Meara seemed to want her to do just that.

". . . so I told her, 'With all due respect, I know you are the ranking officer and you've been with Starfleet longer, but that idea is—and I genuinely mean this in the nicest possible way—completely moronic.' I thought she would pitch a fit, and I could see it building, but then she kind of swallowed it back, smiled, and said, 'You know what, Mister Vandella? You're right.' So then we sat down and we came up with a fix that really works."

"That's great, Stanley," Tikolo said. She had come late, and Vandella had started his dinner before she'd arrived. When he saw her enter the mess, he waved her over. Now he was almost finished, and she had barely begun. Her duty shift would begin in an hour, while Stanley was in the middle of his.

"Cooperation really does pay dividends," he said. He set his fork on his empty plate. "I mean, yes, I would love to have everything my way all the time. Who wouldn't? But that's no way to run a starship, is it?"

"I suppose not." Tikolo forked a piece of baked potato into her mouth.

"I hate to eat and run, darling," Vandella said. "But I have to get back to my duty station. Making progress with the boss doesn't help if you blow it by coming back from dinner late. I'll see you later, won't I?"

"No doubt," Tikolo said. She smiled and gave his hand a squeeze, then watched him leave.

She continued eating, alone at the table, picking up snatches of other conversations. She was not alone for long, though; minutes after Stanley left, she saw Paul O'Meara carrying a tray of food and scanning the room. He spotted her and headed straight toward her. "Is this seat taken?"

"It's all yours," she said. "I'm just about done, though."

He scooted back the chair that Vandella had vacated, put his meal down on the table. "No problem. Any time with you is better than time without." He sat, drawing his chair in close. His foot brushed hers under the table, casually—but, she was convinced, not by accident.

"That's sweet," she said.

"Just the truth."

"How's your day been, Paul?"

"Better now."

The truth was, most security shifts on board the *Enterprise* were boring. The ship was like a small town, and as in any small town, there were disagreements that grew into fights, and there was the constant vigilance required in any controlled situation. But for the most part, the security crew was there to deal with the unusual, with emergency situations. They accompanied landing parties, they handled lawbreakers and attempts against the ship from without. They were assigned to "escort" dignitaries aboard ship, but that was to keep them out of areas they didn't belong. Those things didn't happen often, so they spent the rest of their time trying to stay sharp and prepared for when they did.

O'Meara's plate was heaped with something Tikolo didn't recognize, but he attacked it with gusto. The fare served up by the galley crew was still largely food from Earth, as most of the ship's crew came from there. But they added new and exotic dishes all the time, reflecting the diversity of Starfleet. Whatever O'Meara was eating looked to Tikolo like a heap of worms scooped out of the earth and served under a gritty yellow sauce, and she supposed it was quite the delicacy on Vulcan or Alpha 177 or someplace.

"What are you doing later?" he asked between mouthfuls.

"Working. Then probably sleeping. Eating, working again."

"You have to have some awake time in there somewhere. You need to have some fun, Miranda. All work and no play isn't healthy."

"I didn't say I never played."

"I know. I'm just trying to pin you down to a specific time or activity."

"We're eating together now," she said. "Isn't that good enough?"

"Never good enough. I want to see more of you."

"There's only so much of me to see, Paul."

"You spread yourself thin. You spend time with Stanley and what's-her-name, Ari, and—"

"I like people! A lot of different people. Is that a bad thing?"

"Not in the abstract, no. But there's only so much time in the day, so much time in a life. When there's somebody who's really special, somebody you could make a life with—"

She interrupted before he could go too far. "I haven't found that, Paul. I thought I had, once, but you know what happened. I'd love to find it again. But I'm not there yet."

"I just want to know there's a chance, Miranda. I think we could have a future, and I just need—"

"You need something I can't give you," she said, cutting him off again. "You need some kind of guarantee? I can't do that. I like being with you. Most of the time. Not so much right this minute, though."

O'Meara's fork clanked against his plate. Tikolo found him handsome, liked his high cheekbones and strong jaw and clear green eyes. But now his brow was furrowed and his lips were twisted into a scowl. "I'm not sure how long I can keep going this way, Miranda."

"You don't have to," Tikolo said, anger welling up inside her. "You can't change me, Paul. You are only in charge of yourself. If you don't like the situation, you can wait or you can do something about the aspect of it you can control."

He held his gaze on her for a full minute without speaking. His hands were trembling and his face had turned a couple of shades darker than usual. Then he gathered his utensils and plate and stood up so quickly he almost knocked over his chair. "I love you, Miranda. That doesn't have to mean anything to you, and I guess it doesn't. But it's how I feel, and you'll just have to get used to that."

Before she could respond, he stormed away, dropping his dishes off on an unoccupied table before passing through the door.

Everybody in the mess was looking at her. A couple of people made supportive comments, and within another minute or so, they returned to their own conversations, their private concerns. But the tone of the room was different, as if the floor had been strewn with eggshells nobody wanted to step on.

Tikolo looked at her plate, suddenly not so hungry. She didn't look up again until a pleasant female voice said, "Mind if I join you?"

Tikolo managed a smile for Christine Chapel, who served in sickbay as a nurse. "Be my guest."

The nurse took the seat O'Meara and Vandella had occupied. She didn't have a meal, just a hot drink in a mug, steam circling its rim as if held there by magnets, or gravity. "You okay?" she asked. Her hair was like spun gold catching sunlight, her eyes a piercing blue that Tikolo thought could see through anything.

"Sure. I mean . . ."

"That looked like a pretty emotional scene, is why I ask."

"If you're worried about me medically, or psychologically—"

"I'm off duty, Miranda. I'm worried about you because you're a person."

Tikolo felt the defensive wall she had put up start to slip away. "Thanks," she said. "I guess I'm okay. It's just . . . why do people have to make things so complicated?"

"The eternal question."

"I mean, I can handle myself in a fight. I can deal with the various traumas of interstellar travel. The only thing I can't seem to figure out is what people want. Or, no, not that." She knew what Paul O'Meara wanted. The same thing Stanley Vandella did: some kind of commitment, of exclusivity. They each wanted to be the only romantic or sexual interest in her life.

And she couldn't give either of them that. They wanted a future with her, and since her time on Outpost 4, she was no longer certain there would be a future. Anybody could die at any moment. If it wasn't the Romulans it would be the Klingons, or somebody else. The threat could even be homegrown—humans had never had a hard time coming up with reasons to hate one another.

"I guess what I don't get is why people can't just be happy with what they've got, instead of always wanting more, more, *more*. You give them one piece of you and they want the next one. Give them that and they want the next."

"All people?"

"Most of them, it seems. Men especially, but not just."

"Human nature?" Chapel offered. "The collecting urge runs deep in people. Some more than others, but it's a rare individual who doesn't squirrel away one thing or another."

"Not me," Tikolo said. "I guess, after . . . well, you know, what I went through, I felt like I didn't want to own anything I couldn't carry in both hands, if I needed to leave someplace. I mean, I have my uniforms, my weapons, all the standard gear, but if I had to abandon it all tomorrow, that would be okay."

"You're not alone in that," Chapel said. "But I expect it's rare."

"Do you think it's wrong? A problem or, I don't know, a symptom of a problem?"

"Do you?"

"Now you sound like Doctor McCoy. When he

talks to me, it seems like he always answers my questions with more questions."

"Sorry," Chapel said. "That's our psychological training coming out. It's a way of drawing out the subject."

"But you said—"

"I know." Chapel offered a warm smile. "I said I'm off duty. So I'll just answer your question. I don't think it's bad, or a problem. It might have to do with what you went through—almost certainly, it does. But I think it's a very human response to something like that. And at a guess, I'd say it signifies something deeper."

"Like what?"

"Well, I'm just speculating here, based on the conversations we've had, what I know about you. So I might be way off base."

"I'll let you know if you are."

"Sounds good. Here goes. Your experience left you with a deep-seated uncertainty. You lived, when everyone around you died. You must have had a few 'why me?' moments after that. What would be really troubling is if you didn't."

"Oh, trust me, I've had those."

"And the way you cope with that uncertainty is to live for the now, for the moment. Tomorrow will take care of itself, if it comes at all. Today's acts might have future consequences, but since those can't be known, they can't be avoided. Does that sound right?"

"Right? It sounds like you've been reading my mind."

"Not at all," Chapel said. "Just making some educated guesses."

"I never put it in those terms, but yes. That's really true."

The nurse sipped from her mug. The steam had dissipated, but a spicy aroma drifted across the table. Tikolo thought about Chapel's words, her observation, and how they applied to O'Meara and Vandella.

She didn't want to hurt them, or anyone else. She wanted friends and she wanted lovers. But none of them could be the one and only, and none could claim all her tomorrows. She had not always felt that way, but she did now. If that meant her experience at Outpost 4 had changed something inside her, then so be it. She was who she was.

"Thank you, Nurse Chapel," she said after a few minutes. "For the insight."

"I hope it's helpful," Chapel said. "And please, call me Christine."

"Okay, Christine. Thanks."

"You're welcome. If you'd like to talk, anytime—on or off duty—just say the word."

"I will."

Chapel graced her with another one of those smiles, then rose and left the table. Tikolo finished her meal, feeling better about herself than she had in a long while. She reported for her shift, and she tried to hold at bay any further concerns about her mental or emotional health. She was young and she was alive.

That would just have to do.

"I have a theory, Captain," Spock announced.

Kirk was standing by the viewscreen, staring at the anomaly, ever-changing except for the cluster of ships that appeared cemented in its center. Spock had been sitting quietly at the science station, the rest of the bridge crew attending to their tasks without speaking, and the Vulcan's voice sounded loud in the quiet space, startling.

"We're all ears, Mister Spock," Kirk said. "What is it?"

"I have, as you know, been studying the anomaly, to the extent that our instrumentation will allow."

"And you've reached a conclusion?"

"Several, in fact. The first is that we will not know anything definitive until we are inside it."

"Inside, Mister Spock?"

Was that a ghost of a smile flickering across Spock's face? Impossible to be sure, but it might have been. "Surely you would not readily pass up such a singular opportunity to explore the unknown."

"Should I remind you, Mister Spock, that we're engaged in a diplomatic mission with a critical time-table?"

"Do you think I might have forgotten?"

"Never mind. Carry on."

"The anomaly can best be described, although not with absolute precision, as a dimensional fold."

"Explain."

"Physics describes a number of dimensions—more than twelve, but the precise number is uncertain, because by their very nature some dimensions resist being counted or catalogued. Several of them we all interact with on a regular basis; the most common, of course, being the three dimensions of physical space. Imagine, if you would, those common dimensions, and others less easily conceived of, as flat planes. Infinite in every other respect, but having no variation in height."

"I think we've got it, Mister Spock," Kirk said. "Perfectly flat."

"Yes, Captain. A dozen or more flat planes. Now imagine that they are all slightly skewed, and they all intersect one another."

"I think I have it," Chekov said. He sounded excited. Kirk liked the young man, but boyish enthusiasm occasionally lost its charm.

"Very well," Spock said. "Now take your mental image of those intersecting planes, right at the point where they do intersect, and . . . fold it."

"Fold it?" Uhura asked.

"Fold it."

"I'm folding," Uhura said. "It's making my head hurt."

"Aside from that, what would you surmise, Lieutenant?" Spock asked.

"These dimensions," Uhura said, "they don't connect the way they ordinarily would."

"That is correct."

"Because, for instance," Kirk said, holding his hands perpendicular, his right bisecting the palm of his left, "while depth and width usually relate like so . . ." He wrapped his hands around each other. ". . . you're saying that in there, it's more like this."

"The word 'fold' lacks a certain specificity," Spock admitted. "But again, because of the nature of what we are discussing, I doubt that we could do better. Your demonstration, Captain, is as good as any. Only try to imagine not just the three dimensions we know as Euclidean space being folded together, but also time and the other dimensions not so easily conceived."

"Now *my* head hurts," Kirk said. "What you're describing would make . . . no sense."

"Not in any traditional way, no."

"But it's possible?" Sulu asked. "That sort of fold?"

"Nothing that is impossible can exist," Spock said. "This exists; therefore, it is possible."

Kirk could tell by the tone of Spock's voice that he would rather not have to admit that the fold was real. For his own part, he wished that he could wake up and have it be part of a bad dream, because the more Spock described it, the less he liked the idea of venturing inside. "And the *McRaven* happened to fly right into it," he said.

"We might have as well," Uhura reminded him. "If we hadn't been reducing speed because we knew we were getting close to the *McRaven*. At warp speed, by the time we'd noticed that our instruments were acting up, it would have been too late."

"And without instruments, getting out could be impossible. Whatever else it might be," Sulu added, "it's a most effective trap."

The captain thought about the dozens of ships seen in the magnified view of the anomaly—the dimensional fold—all clustered around the single, huge ship at its center. "So it seems," he said. "Mister Spock, can you tell us anything about conditions inside the fold?"

"One can only guess," Spock replied. "It would be safe to say that it would be like nothing any of us have experienced before. Without being inside it, I can speculate that the dimensions do not function in their typical manner, but I cannot begin to say precisely what that would mean. I cannot even say with any certainty that someone inside the fold would be able to comprehend the environment. It might, in fact, drive one mad."

"Are you suggesting that we not go into it?" Kirk said.

"I am merely suggesting that we be forewarned when we do go into it."

"Are there any precautions we can take?"

"None that I am aware of."

"Are you sure entering the fold is a good idea, Captain?" Uhura asked.

"Not at all," Kirk said. "But I've acted on bad ideas before, and I'm still here. Sometimes a bad idea is all I've got. This just might be one of those times."

Seven

"We do not know if all humans are as stubborn as Kirk," Minister Chan'ya said. "He maddens us." She sat with her retinue in her private quarters, speaking in her native Ixtoldan, which was full of harsh gutturals and hard consonants, not at all like the language spoken on the *Enterprise*. Their tongue was smooth, making it, she believed, a good language for lies but not for much else.

"Do we feel that he's a danger, Minister?" Keneseth asked. He was the smallest of the group aside from Chan'ya herself, with a fine face, a mouth full of sharp teeth, and narrow, gold-flecked eyes that seemed to see all, never betraying a moment's weakness. His voice was deep and commanding, and Chan'ya sometimes wished he used it more often. She understood, however, that when he finally did speak, others listened. "We could take steps."

"We don't feel that is necessary," Chan'ya said. She knew what steps he had in mind, and they wouldn't win any friends with the Federation Council. "Not at this time. Perhaps, later . . ."

Keneseth lowered his eyelids once, in affirmation.

Chan'ya turned to the others at the table: Skanderen, Cris'ya, Antelis, and Tre'aln. "When, Minister? If he goes in to explore the ships, he might—"

"We know what he *might* do! We can only react to what he does. Need we remind us what is at stake here?"

"No, Minister," Tre'aln said, chastened. "We are aware of the importance of the situation."

"Then trust us also to be aware," Chan'ya said, rising from her chair. Even standing, she was barely taller than the seated Cris'ya. She clenched her right fist and slapped it against her other palm, lightly but, she believed, with dramatic impact. "Well and good. We yet have options. As long as we are here, and the *Ton'bey* is nearby, there are steps that can be taken. Just know this—those steps *will* be taken, if necessary, whatever the cost to us. At this, we cannot fail, and we will not fail. This we swear."

"Well, you canna beam over, that's for sure. Who knows what you'd be on the other side?"

Kirk had summoned Spock and Scotty into his quarters for a private discussion about how best to reach the *McRaven*. Scotty was ticking off on his fingers the methods that wouldn't work.

Kirk had already written off the idea of using the transporter. They had learned, not that long ago, that transporter technology could go awry under certain circumstances—though he did think Spock looked good with a goatee. Beaming into an environment in which the normal rules of physics didn't apply seemed like an invitation to disaster.

They had similarly decided against taking the *Enterprise* into the fold, since they had no way to control the fold's effects on the ship's instrumentation, and being trapped there, like the *McRaven,* was exactly the fate they were trying to avoid.

"I do have one idea, Captain," Scotty said. "It's risky as the dickens, but it might work."

"Don't worry about the risk," Kirk said. He was mostly joking, but not entirely. "Chances are we won't survive the trip anyway."

Scotty ignored the comment, which was exactly the response it deserved. "Here 'tis," he said. "We send a shuttle. Instead of relying on its own propulsion and other systems, which won't work once it's inside, I'll engineer the tractor beam to work in reverse. It'll repel the shuttle, pushing it on a defined course instead of drawing it in. If anything goes wrong, I'll just switch back to tractor mode and pull it free."

"It could work. Opinions, Mister Spock?"

"Of the various ideas offered so far, that appears to be the least bad," Spock said.

"Of course," Kirk said, "once we're inside the fold, there are no guarantees. The tractor beam might be as affected by the dimensional chaos as anything else."

"True," Spock said. "And we have no certainty that any momentum achieved would continue as anticipated. Whatever gravitational pull that big star-ship exerts, however, would most likely draw us in the rest of the way."

"Then our only problem would be getting back."

"Correct."

"There are electrical impulses on that big ship," Kirk said. "They're faint, but who knows how life-forms might read to our instruments from within that dimensional crazy quilt. For all we know, we could be picking up traces of the *McRaven*'s crew."

"Captain, you're not sayin' that *you'll* be making the bloody trip, without even knowing you'll be able to get back."

"I'm counting on you to figure something out while I'm gone, Scotty."

"Sir—"

"I'll know you'll find a way."

A broad smile spread across the engineer's face. "It's what I do."

Kirk and Spock were on the bridge plotting out the specifics with Sulu, Uhura, and Chekov when Chan'ya showed up, accompanied by Gonzales, Perkins, and Rinaldo.

"Captain Kirk," Gonzales said. "We were hoping to find you here."

"What can I do for you?" Kirk asked.

"Minister Chan'ya would like to know if there's been a decision about the *McRaven*."

"You know our decision, Minister. The only open question has been how to get to the ship, and we believe we've solved that."

"The mission will be conducted in a time-sensitive manner, we trust," Chan'ya said.

"If there are survivors on that ship, I want to reach them as soon as possible, yes. But if we do find any, then we'll have to work out how to get them safely back to the *Enterprise*, and that might take some time." He had to work to keep the exasperation out of his voice. "You've heard all this before, Minister. Nothing has changed except that we've figured out how to get there."

"We understand, Captain," Chan'ya said. Her skin was a darker red than he had ever seen it. "We merely hope to encourage the utmost speed. We would rather you accept that it is too late to help anyone on board that ship and continue on to Ixtolde. But if you refuse—"

"I do."

"Well and good. We will file our protest with the Federation and wish for a speedy and successful conclusion to what we feel is an unnecessary and ill-conceived venture."

Ill-conceived? You don't know the half of it, Kirk thought. "Thank you," he said.

Chan'ya turned and headed for the turbolift. Kirk was getting used to the move, always executed with the same impatient air. The others followed her. This time, however, Perkins hung back. He approached Kirk with urgency in his eyes.

"Captain," he said quietly. "May I meet with you and your command staff?" He glanced toward the turbolift. The door had opened and Chan'ya and the others had stepped on. "It's urgent. Say, fifteen minutes in your briefing room?"

"Fifteen minutes," Kirk echoed.

Perkins turned toward his colleagues. "Thank you, Captain," he said loudly as he made for the turbolift, covering himself. "I'll visit there, when I have the opportunity."

"What was that about, Captain?" Spock asked when the door had closed.

"I have no idea," Kirk answered. "But we won't have to wait long to find out."

Eight

"There aren't any giants, you know," Gillayne said. She and Aleshia were huddled beneath a tin roof, with rain hammering down on it so loud they almost had to shout to be heard. The rain had wet the dry landscape enough to release the locked-in aromas of the plants, sweetening the air against the other, more predominant stink. Where the rain struck the bodies of those who had fallen, it sizzled, and the bubbling flesh gave off a rancid stench, so anything that diluted it was welcome.

"What do you mean?" Aleshia asked. She'd heard rumors before, of course. But her father swore giants were real, and so did Kalso and Yignay and the other elders.

"Just that. It's not giants. Same as this rain is not rain at all."

Aleshia looked at where the rain spilled off the roof's lowest corner and pooled on the ground, yellow and frothy. This was not typical rainwater, that much was true. "What, then? Is it not wet?"

"Wet, yes," Gillayne said, tugging at her gray shift, which had been torn, patched, and torn again. "But did you see the clouds gathering before it fell? They were pure white, not dark like the ones that bring rain. And they formed in minutes, not hours."

"But . . . Father said—"

"We've been lied to our whole lives, Aleshia. That's nothing new."

"How do you know, then?"

"I asked."

"Asked who?"

"Margyan," Gillayne said. She spoke the name so softly that Aleshia strained to hear. But she understood the reason. Nobody spoke of Margyan, not where others could hear. Some called her a wise woman, others a sorceress, but none of them liked her. The villagers let her stay because she spent money in their shops and because nobody was sure how she might react to banishment.

"You saw her?"

"Two nights ago, in the dark, I went to her house."

"You didn't! Alone?"

"Of course alone, do you think I'm mad?"

"But—"

"I had questions. I knew she would have answers."

"And she told you things?"

"What did you think she would do? Eat me?"

"Perhaps. What are they, then, if not giants?"

"She isn't certain. But it is no accident, she says, that people die each time. Same with the rain. They're trying to reduce our numbers, she says. Cut us down."

"Why, Gillayne?"

"Why fill our heads with lies? They want to keep us stupid. Well, ignorant. So we won't know how to fight back, she says. So we'll keep selling them our crops and livestock for a pittance."

"Who? The cities?"

"According to Margyan, even the cities are ruled by someone else."

Aleshia's head was too cluttered with the things Gillayne was saying. It was as though her friend were giving her a hundred threads, all unspooled, and she couldn't grasp the end of even one of them and follow it all the way. "But then, why kill us?"

"They're coming for us, she says. Won't be long, now."

"How does she know all this? And why doesn't anyone else?"

"She says she knows because she watches and listens. As for why the rest don't know—maybe they do. Maybe they just refuse to see—or to admit that they do know."

"And who is it who's coming for us? Who rules the city-dwellers, according to her?"

Gillayne swung a hand toward the sky. "Them! The ones who stay away."

"There is so much I don't understand," Aleshia said.

"Talk to Margyan, then. She is friendlier than people say. She's lonely."

"She looks so—"

"What? Haggard? Worn out? If you had lived the life she has, why, you would look that way, too."

"I'll go then," Aleshia said. "To Margyan's. I want to know the truth. I *need* to know it."

"You were always like that," Gillayne said. "Even as a little girl."

"Well, I haven't changed, then." Aleshia looked at the rain, pattering against the ground, dissolving the carcasses of those caught out in it. *When will it end?* she wondered. She was hungry; she and Gillayne had been trapped under the metal roof for hours.

She would wait a while longer. As long as it took.

If Gillayne was right—or if Margyan was—then every hour underneath a roof of tin was, at least, one more hour of life. And those, it seemed, might be fewer all the time.

Kirk and Spock went to the briefing room. McCoy joined them there a couple of minutes later, and Kirk laid out the plan for him.

"Jim—" McCoy said.

"Bones, we've got to get to that ship, and there's no other way to do it."

"It sounds like suicide, Jim."

"That's why I'm going alone."

"The hell you are!"

"The doctor is right, Captain," Spock said. "You are the commander of this ship. You cannot go, alone or otherwise."

"I will not order anyone else to undertake a mission like this."

"Jim—"

The doctor's protestation was cut off by the door buzzer. "Come," Kirk said.

The door whooshed open and Perkins stepped inside quickly. "Thank you for seeing me," he said.

Kirk waved to the empty chairs around the table. "Have a seat."

The Federation diplomat shook his head. He was a walking bundle of nerves. He had a soft, round face, unlined and devoid of hair. His body was also soft and round, his clothes billowing like balloons mostly full of water. His eyes darted this way and that, as if watching for pursuers. A thin sheen of sweat coated his face. "You can speak freely in here," Kirk assured him. "Our privacy is assured."

"Gonzales would kill me if he knew I was here."

"Nobody's getting killed," Kirk said. "Now, what did you want to see us about?"

Perkins paced about the room as he spoke. "It's what they won't tell you," he said.

"Gonzales?"

"Yes, and Minister Chan'ya. She knows, but I don't know that the rest of her party does. It's classified, you see. Very, very classified."

"Above my level?" Kirk asked.

"I'm afraid so, yes."

"But you're going to tell me anyway? You

understand what the consequences of that could be."

"I do. But I also understand the possible consequences of *not* telling you. That's not something I'm willing to do."

"All right, then," Kirk said. "What is it we need to know?"

"The *McRaven*'s mission," Perkins said.

"I admit I have wondered about that. It seemed to be headed toward Ixtolde."

"It is. Was, rather."

"To what end?" Spock asked.

"Do you know the name Albert Tsien D'Asaro?"

"It doesn't ring any bells," Kirk said.

"An inventor," Spock said. "From Rouen, France, on Earth."

"That's right," Perkins said, obviously surprised and impressed at Spock's knowledge. "More recently of Muscatine, Iowa, in North America. He has worked on methods of increasing crop productivity that repair and enhance soil rather than leaching the nutrients from it. He is not well known, but he is highly respected in his field, and he has many friends on the Federation Council. He's been appointed ambassador to Ixtolde."

"But Ixtolde's Federation membership isn't confirmed yet," Kirk said.

"Right again. That's why his trip was so secret. While all the attention was focused on the *Enterprise*, he was going ahead of us, to get a head start learning the Ixtoldan language, their customs, the lay of the land, if you will. The idea was that when they were confirmed—which everyone believes is just a matter of time—he would be ahead of the game. And his particular scientific skills might help Ixtolde, since they've had issues with widespread famine there. The Council hoped he could help with that quickly, before another growing season passes."

"So if he doesn't make it—"

"If he doesn't make it, the Federation will appoint a new ambassador. But the schedule will be thrown off, the growing season will come and go, and potentially thousands of Ixtoldans will die before we can get somebody else there with his background and knowledge. He was the right man for the job, and the urgency is extreme."

"Who knows about this?" Kirk asked.

"Just Minister Chan'ya. She's the one who set it up with the Ixtoldan government."

"But she's been pushing us from the beginning to abandon the *McRaven* and hurry on to Ixtolde."

Perkins let out a sigh that seemed to bubble from deep within. "I can't pretend that I understand the minister's agenda. I suspect that what she puts first is Minister Chan'ya, and every other consideration comes in a distant second."

"Are you saying that she's workin' against the interests of her own people?" McCoy asked.

"Not necessarily," Perkins replied. He chewed on

his lower lip for a moment. "I don't always understand how her goals line up with theirs, that's all. But there's so much about Ixtolde that I don't know—that none of us know. That's part of why D'Asaro was going there ahead of us, and the entire reason for our trip. Minister Chan'ya's actions might come into clearer focus after we know more about the place and its inhabitants. For now, I'm as much in the dark as you are. I just thought you needed to know that the ambassador is on that ship."

"I appreciate that, Mister Perkins," Kirk said. "And I'll do everything I can to get him safely off it." *If*, he left unsaid, *it's not already too late. We can only hope to reach it in time.*

When Perkins was gone, Kirk turned to the others. "Now do you agree that I have to go?"

"It still could be somebody else, Jim," Bones said. "It doesn't have to be you."

"I disagree. My first responsibility is to the Federation, not just to the *Enterprise*. If the Council is concerned about potential famine on Ixtolde and has sent someone to help avert it, then I have to do whatever I can to make sure that he gets there."

"The ambassador is probably dead," Spock pointed out. "Those electrical impulses are faint and likely do not represent organic life-forms."

"But we don't know that," Kirk insisted. "We don't know how the unknown nature of the fold affects what our instruments are picking up. And we won't until we go there in person and find out."

"As the ship's science officer," Spock said, "I must point out this is a unique opportunity to study a phenomenon never before encountered. I must insist on accompanying any mission into the dimensional fold."

McCoy planted his palm against his forehead. "Well, if you've both gone nuts, I guess I gotta go over, too, just to keep an eye on you. There's gotta be somebody sane along, to make sure you two survive the trip!"

Kirk started to respond, but stopped himself before he got a word out. He gave his answer another moment's thought. Finally, he said, "I guess that's settled, then. The three of us, and a security team. All volunteers—nobody gets ordered onto a mission like this. I wouldn't say it's certain suicide . . . in fact, I wouldn't say there's anything the least bit certain about any of it. Except, perhaps, for uncertainty. That, I'm pretty sure, is the one thing we can count on."

Nine

Miranda Tikolo was one of the first to volunteer when Captain Kirk announced the landing party. She wanted to get away—away from the ship, away from Paul O'Meara and Stanley Vandella and Ari Bevilaqua. Of the three, Bevilaqua was the least demanding, the most willing to let Tikolo be herself, without expecting her to devote all her time and energy to just one relationship. Bevilaqua was easy to be with, comfortable as old, broken-in shoes.

But the petty officer wanted distance from her, too. She needed time to think, and space in which to do it. So she signed up for what the captain stressed would be a very dangerous mission. She made it down to the hangar deck with time to spare, moving awkwardly in the environmental suit they had been ordered to wear, and watched the engineering crew preparing two shuttles for service. She was engrossed in the preparations when she heard a familiar voice behind her.

"Miranda," Vandella said. Like her, he wore an environmental suit, and carried his helmet under his arm. "I am delighted to see that we'll both be on this mission. It sounds like an exciting one, doesn't it?"

"You didn't know I'd volunteered?"

"How could I?"

She didn't say anything, but she noted that he had not actually answered her question. And the real answer was, there were any number of ways he could have known, including simply asking the captain or any of his staff, or checking the sign-up log, or speaking with someone who had been there when she'd agreed to the mission. The fact that he had dodged the question meant he would likely dodge her follow-up, which would have been, "Did you volunteer just because you knew I did?"

But she didn't ask it, because the doors opened and another group stepped into the hangar deck, including Captain Kirk, Commander Spock, and Doctor McCoy. "Oh, joyous," Vandella said, sarcasm fairly dripping off the words.

"What?" she started to ask. But then Paul O'Meara stepped out from behind Spock and McCoy. From his angle, Vandella had been able to see him first.

"Oh," she said.

O'Meara strode up to them and stopped before Miranda, a smile pasted to his face that looked every bit artificial. "Miranda," he said. "Stanley. What a surprise."

"Well, given what the captain said about the circumstances, I felt I could hardly decline. Apparently we all felt that way."

"Looks like," O'Meara said.

"If this is going to be a problem—" Tikolo began.

"No problem," O'Meara said. "The captain needs backup. That's what we do."

"That's exactly right," Vandella added. "I know there's some . . . rivalry, here . . . but we are professionals, after all. Whatever our feelings for you, they needn't interfere with our duty."

"They'd better not," Tikolo said. She wanted to trust him, to trust them both. But trust was hard to come by lately. She suspected it had to do with her trauma. Before that, she had been able to love and trust Eric Rockwell completely, and after, those feelings seemed like distant memories, like dreams that dissipated upon waking, no more easily grasped than a fistful of water.

"All right," she said, relenting. She didn't like it—part of her reason for volunteering for the mission had been to be away from these two, to get a change of scenery, see some different faces. But they were right. They were professionals. Landing parties were a crucial part of the job.

Before she had a chance to say anything more, the captain addressed the group and everybody fell silent. "Thank you for being here. I told you before you signed on that this would be a dangerous mission. I need to stress that. There's a possibility that none of us will make it back here. Of course, I believe we will.

"The *Enterprise* has been in tough places before. Some have given their lives for this ship, and we all knew what the risks were when we enlisted. That said, I'm looking at this as a rescue mission. We'll be counting on you to keep yourselves and each other safe, and to do the same for anyone we find on the *McRaven*. We don't know what we're going to encounter when we get into what Mister Spock calls the 'dimensional fold,' but on the way over, he'll explain what he has been able to deduce about it. And, as I told you up front, we're not entirely sure how we're going to be able to get back to the *Enterprise*. We have an idea— we just won't know if it will work until we try it. You can still back out now if you want. I'll understand completely if you do."

For a brief instant, the idea of taking the out the captain had offered flitted through Tikolo's mind. Sending Vandella and O'Meara into the dimensional fold, whatever that was, would have the same effect as her going in without them. She would be away from them for a while, free of their constant pressure, able to think things through more clearly.

But she couldn't make a decision like that on such a purely personal basis. This was duty, and she owed Captain Kirk her loyalty and her service. She stayed put.

So did the eleven other volunteers. She had expected no less.

"I guess that's settled, then," Kirk said after a moment. "Helmets on. Let's get this show on the road, shall we?"

The away team secured their helmets, split into two groups, and boarded the shuttles. Tikolo joined the group getting into the second, forcing O'Meara and Vandella to ride in the first, without her. They would just have to fend for themselves; she wasn't going to make it easy for them to get in the way of her alone-time.

Christine Chapel looked up from the computer screen, letting her gaze float toward the ceiling as she tried to wrap her thoughts around what she had learned. She sat that way for only a few moments, though; there was an obvious urgency to the information, and it had to be shared with Doctor McCoy as soon as possible. She only hoped she wasn't too late. She punched the sickbay's intercom controls and paged Doctor McCoy, but instead of his voice, Uhura reported back. *"His shuttle has just left the hangar deck,"* the voice said. *"Do you want me to patch you through?"*

"No, thank you," she said. Cutting the connection, she added, "Damn it all!"

"What's wrong?" Neola Aimenthe asked. She was a medical assistant who was helping Chapel in sickbay.

"Oh, I was hoping to catch him before he boarded the shuttle. I don't want to talk to him there—they're so small, and there's no privacy. People are entitled to have their medical records kept private."

"Of course," Aimenthe said. She was small and

dark, with eyes that might have appeared furtive in a less open face. As it was, they made her look lively, if a little unfocused. But she knew her medicine, and Chapel thought she'd make a fine ship's doctor one of these days. "It's about a patient?"

"Miranda Tikolo," Chapel said.

"Oh, she's nice. Troubled, though."

"That's not the half of it," Chapel said. "What I just learned . . ."

"What?"

Chapel hesitated. Aimenthe was part of the medical team, just as much as she was. She hadn't been around for as long as Chapel or Doctor McCoy, but that didn't mean she couldn't be trusted. "I'm not even sure Tikolo knows, herself. I doubt that she does, in fact."

"Knows what? You make it all sound so mysterious."

Chapel let out a sigh and tapped the top of the computer. "When she was just a year old, her parents divorced. Her mother remarried, fairly quickly, and her father—I suspect this was one of the issues that caused marital problems in the first place—had a psychotic break. Miranda was not quite three years old. She was home one night with her mother, her new stepfather, and her older stepbrothers and sister. Her biological father came to their home, enraged. He had a knife hidden in his coat. The stepfather opened the door, and Miranda's father slashed his throat. He stepped over the man and into the house. His ex-wife charged but he buried the knife in her eye, straight to the brain. Then he started in on the kids."

"That's awful!" Aimenthe said. She had her fist up in front of her mouth. "I mean, awful doesn't begin to describe it, but—"

"I know," Chapel said. "I'm not sure there are words in our language, or any other. The stepsister grabbed little Miranda, who was just a toddler, and carried her into a bedroom. She hid her in a closet, behind some coats, and closed the door. When she got back into the main room, her brothers were both dead. She was next."

"And Miranda?"

"I'm coming to that. A neighbor noticed three days later that he hadn't seen anyone in the family, and he called the authorities. They discovered the bodies, and found Miranda in the closet. Her father confessed as soon as they approached him. He said he didn't know where the toddler had been hidden, and he was afraid to spend any time looking. He would have killed her, too. Miranda had not budged from the closet for those three days, and she didn't talk for seven weeks after that. But she didn't seem to remember anything about what had happened, didn't remember the murders, her father, anything. That night was a complete blank for her. As far as I can find out, she's never been told. The records were sealed because she was so young. She was adopted soon after, by the Tikolo family, and they never even told her they weren't her biological parents."

"You're kidding."

"It's a sensitive issue. Especially combined with early childhood trauma, although there's no indication that they even knew precisely what she had been through. Anyway, she didn't appear to suffer any long-term effects from it, and it never made it into her Starfleet files, nor was it referenced in her psych evals. I put it together from press accounts and court records."

"You said they're sealed."

"Any seal can be broken," Chapel said with a smile. "You just have to have the right keys. I know this guy . . ."

"You don't have to say any more," Aimenthe said. "I get it."

"He's just a friend. Point is, Miranda Tikolo has suffered far more psychological damage than she even knows about. She thinks she's okay with what happened to her off Outpost 4, and maybe she is. Then again—"

"Maybe she's not."

"Right."

"You should try to get word to Doctor McCoy, if you can do it discreetly."

"I will. In the meantime, I guess we just have to hope that she doesn't suffer any more trauma. Poor thing's had more than enough for one lifetime."

"You know, Jim," McCoy said quietly as he settled into his shuttle seat. "If we do find survivors over there—"

"We'll have to figure out how to get them back to the *Enterprise,* on these shuttles," Kirk finished for him. "I know, Bones. I don't know what the answer is. I'm hoping that we'll learn enough about the anomaly by going into it to come up with the solution."

The problem had been nagging at him ever since they'd come up with the idea of pushing shuttles in from outside. Even that plan was questionable at best, since there was no way to know what would happen to the shuttles once they entered the fold.

As a test, they had removed the explosive combination of matter and antimatter from a photon torpedo and launched it into the fold, and it seemed to follow its ordinary trajectory with only a few minor wobbles. The ship's instruments had lost track of it once it entered the fold, though, and the bridge crew had lost visual contact, regained it, then lost it again, for good. Spock had pointed out that without any passengers on board, there was no way to know what a sentient being would have experienced as the torpedo journeyed on what appeared to be a fairly straight course into the anomaly. Moving a physical object through space was one thing—moving through warped dimensions, possibly other realities, was something entirely different.

They were venturing into the unknown in a way that hadn't been done since Zefram Cochrane took his first warp flight, on the fifth of April in 2063. That flight had brought Earth to the attention of the

Vulcans and the larger community of the galaxy. Who knew where this one might lead?

Outside, the hangar deck had been depressurized, and the shuttles started to move. Kirk sat back, still impressed, even after all his experience, with the sensation of motion as the little craft launched into space. It was much more pronounced than he felt inside the *Enterprise*, even at warp speeds. And space looked very, very big from inside a tiny shuttle.

Within a short while, they were clear of the *Enterprise* and could glimpse it diminishing in size behind them. The second shuttle was a bright spot between them and the ship. The vessels locked in the center of the fold loomed larger and larger with every passing minute.

When it seemed that they had almost reached the twisting, shifting, color-phasing interior of the anomaly, Scotty's voice sounded over the speakers. "*It's time to cut your power,*" he said. "*We're ready to give you a push!*"

Bunker, the crewman at the shuttle's helm, turned back toward Kirk. "Sir?"

"Cut the engines," Kirk ordered.

"Aye, sir." He did. The steady drone of the shuttle's engines vanished. Now Kirk felt doubly vulnerable, in a tiny craft under no power at all.

"Engines are off, Mister Scott," Bunker declared. He had a rugged face, and silver threads shooting through his short, dark hair made him look older than he was. But he had the hands of a surgeon, and he knew how to fly a shuttle.

"*Here comes a shove,*" Scotty announced. "*Ye might feel a wee jolt.*"

"Hang on," Kirk warned. He was glad he had. When the tractor beam reached them, the sensation was less a "wee jolt" and more like they'd been rear-ended by a craft twice their size.

"Everybody okay?" he asked when the shuttle had leveled off again.

A chorus of responses in the affirmative reached his ears.

"Mister Scott," Kirk called.

"*Aye, Captain?*"

"When you push the second shuttle, you might want to try a lighter touch, Scotty. Or at the very least, make your warning a little stronger."

"*Sorry, Captain. I didnae mean t' shake everybody up.*"

"Understood. Everything seems fine now. Kirk out."

And everything *was* fine. The tractor beam pushed the shuttle gently through the vacuum of space. Through the forward ports, he could see the kaleidoscope of colors loom larger, signifying that the dimensional fold was growing closer and closer.

"Steady, people," Kirk said. "We're about to go inside, and we haven't the slightest idea what we'll find there."

"What do you think it'll be like, Mister Spock?" someone behind him asked. Kirk thought it was Vandella, but he wasn't certain.

"I am uncertain," Spock replied, "but—"

Before he could finish his thought, the shuttle passed through the boundary of the fold.

Ten

"Captain!" Bunker called. "We've lost all our instruments!"

The comm system speakers crackled with static. Kirk could barely make out Scotty's voice. "*Captain . . . lost you on . . . status . . .*"

"We're fine, Scotty!" Kirk called. He had no idea if his signal would reach the *Enterprise,* but the ship's communication systems were more sophisticated than the shuttle's, so there was a chance. "We're inside the anomaly, but we're fine!"

"Captain," Bunker said again. He sounded beyond anxious. "I've got no control."

"We didn't expect to, Mister Bunker. Steady as she goes."

"I hope everybody's strapped in," Bunker said. "Because we're—"

He couldn't get the rest of his sentence out, but his meaning was obvious. The shuttle was rolling to starboard, fast. Outside, violet lightning carved a jagged streak across Kirk's field of view, burning into his retinas. The light inside the shuttle was a strange shade of pink, flickering toward red near Kirk's fellow passengers, as if they were throwing off energy that altered the light's properties.

He gripped the console, as if that, rather than the straps, would hold him in. Halfway through the roll, the shuttle's artificial gravity cut out. In a way it was a blessing, since it eliminated some of the nausea-making effects of the ship's motion. It had its own drawbacks, though, as everything loose in the shuttle's interior that had started to fall during the roll stopped and floated, bringing some of it back to where it could bump into the passengers. Kirk saw a tricorder heading toward him, and wondered who hadn't secured it.

"It's been a hell of a long time since I've been airsick," McCoy said through clenched teeth. "But this trip just might do it."

Kirk glanced over at Spock. Through his helmet, the Vulcan's flesh looked pale, his lips were clamped shut, his eyebrows arched.

". . . *Kirk . . . read me?*" Scotty's voice demanded. Most of the transmission was lost to static.

"Scotty!" Kirk called. "We're experiencing some . . . turbulence. But the shuttle's intact and we're okay."

"*. . . cap . . . jector . . .*"

"Never mind that, Jim," McCoy said. "He can't hear you and we can't hear him."

The doctor was right. And Kirk had other things to worry about. The shuttle's interior lights flickered twice, then blinked out. At the same instant, the gentle background hum of its climate control system stilled. With it, the voices of the passengers went quiet.

"All systems are down, Captain," Bunker said. "We're dead in the water."

Everybody had an environmental suit on, so their temperature and oxygen needs would be met for a while—if *those* systems continued to work. If not . . . then coming into the dimensional fold was the mistake that many had believed it would be.

"We are on our own," Spock said. "We cannot reach Mister Scott, nor can we warn the second shuttle to turn around."

"Full speed ahead," Kirk said. Then he thought better of his response. "There must be a way to fix this."

"'Fixing' it is beyond our capabilities," Spock said. "The most we can do is hang on and hope."

"Hope?" McCoy echoed. "That's the best you've got?"

"It is the only option available to us at the moment, Doctor."

"Being upset with each other isn't going to help," Kirk said. "And it'll use up your oxygen faster."

"I know, Jim," McCoy said. "Sorry, Spock."

"No apology is required."

"Oh, for Pete's sake, you—"

McCoy stopped in the middle of his sentence, because the shuttle shook as if it had just run into something solid. At the same instant, the interior lights returned, except—*reversed* was the only way Kirk could conceptualize it, like a negative image from an old photographic process. The light being emitted from the fixtures was black, the deepest shadows pure white. Every other surface was a shade of gray: light ones darker and dark ones lighter.

And the shuttle began a reverse of its earlier roll. Halfway through, the artificial gravity kicked in. Floating objects began to fall toward the overhead. Kirk recognized the tricorder, and realized it was in the exact same position he had seen it before. The odds against that happening were astronomical, unless—

The captain glanced at Bones and Spock. They were in precisely the same positions they had been before, their facial expressions identical. Even he was gripping the console in the exact same way.

This was not *like* the earlier roll, in the opposite direction—this *was* the earlier roll, in reverse. They were reliving the moment, backward, with the only difference being his awareness of it.

It couldn't be happening.

But—unless a lack of oxygen was causing him to hallucinate—it was.

When the roll was finished, the lighting returned to normal, much to Kirk's relief. Nearly everyone spoke at once, and Scotty's voice blared from the speakers, still cut by static but not as completely obscured as before. "*canna read you, shut . . . tain, are you . . .*"

"We're okay, Mister Scott," Kirk replied, hoping

that this time the chief engineer could hear him. "Repeat, we're unharmed."

"All systems are back on line," Bunker reported.

"*Roger that, Captain,*" Scotty said. "*I read ye loud and clear that time.*"

"And you, Scotty," Kirk said. "Loud and clear."

Sweat beaded McCoy's forehead. He probably wanted to mop it, but didn't dare remove his helmet. "That's a little better," he said.

"It is indeed," Kirk said. "Theories, Mister Spock?"

"It is possible," Spock replied, "that the effects of the dimensional fold are more pronounced at its edges and that the interior of the fold is more stable. Having passed through what appeared to be a time reversal, we may have seen the worst of it."

"I like the sound of that," McCoy said.

"It is also possible," Spock continued, "that what we are experiencing now is the exception and the other the rule. In which case, all precautionary measures should remain in effect."

"Well, thanks for that," McCoy observed.

"Point taken, Mister Spock," Kirk said. "It appears that our environmental systems are back, but we can't count on them staying that way. Keep your helmets on and be ready for anything."

"Captain," O'Meara said from behind Spock. "Can we contact the second shuttle? See how they're faring?"

"Kirk to engineering," Kirk said. "Scotty, any news on the other shuttle?"

"*We lost 'em as soon as they entered the anomaly,*" Scotty replied. "*Same as we did you.*"

"Give them a minute and then try again," Kirk said. "How's our heading?"

"*You're still on course.*"

"Good."

"*In fact—*"

"Yes?"

"Captain," Bunker interrupted. "We're there."

Eleven

Miranda Tikolo had hoped she might doze off on the shuttle trip. Her sleep the night before had been restless, riven by bad dreams. But stepping onto the shuttle, all the memories of that time off Outpost 4 had come roaring back to her. Her heart rate quickened and she had a hard time drawing breath. She took a seat, grateful to get off suddenly unsteady legs.

"Are you okay?" someone asked. In their environmental suits, everybody looked the same, and Tikolo was having a hard time focusing. Her vision seemed to have narrowed down to a slender tube, with darkness encroaching on every side. The suit felt as if it was squeezing in on her, compressing her chest.

"Fine," she said. "I'm fine. Yeah."

"Because you look a little pale."

"I said I'm fine," Tikolo snapped. "Sorry."

"Okay, okay."

The petty officer strapped herself in. The pressure of the straps made the claustrophobic sensations even worse, but she swallowed her discomfort. There was no way out of it; she had volunteered for the mission, and when the captain had offered an opportunity to back out, she hadn't taken it. She was in it for the duration.

Within a few minutes, everyone had boarded, and the shuttle was in motion, leaving the *Enterprise* behind.

The forward ports were filled with the accumulated starships gathered around the big one in the middle. "Big" didn't actually begin to describe it. The closer they got, the more Kirk realized that it was gigantic, larger by far than any ship he had ever seen. From here, it didn't appear all that impressive from a technological viewpoint—almost primitive, in fact, as if all the effort expended on it had gone into size instead of sophistication.

Some of the ships clustered around it were of recognizable origins. The *McRaven* was clearly visible, dead ahead. Kirk thought another was also a Starfleet ship, though of a class not manufactured for many years. Some of the ships were decaying, seemingly rusted through despite the lack of an atmosphere, and jammed so close together that they seemed to have melted into one another, making identification impossible. He thought he saw a Romulan bird-of-prey, an Andorian cruiser, something that might have been Tholian.

The big ship in the middle, though, was of no genesis Kirk could determine. "Mister Spock, can you determine the planet of origin of that huge ship?"

"No, Captain. I see no familiar markings or technology. In fact, there are no visible markings of any kind."

That was strange in itself. Kirk couldn't recall an example of a completely unmarked starship. This one had scorch stains down its long central section, and visible decay, so it was possible that the markings had simply been worn away by time and the difficulties of its journey. "Anybody have an idea?" he asked.

He heard only negative responses.

"*Captain,*" Scotty's voice boomed over the speakers, almost as loud as if he had been in the shuttle with them. "*The second shuttle's reported in. They had a rough go of it for a while, but they're on course and under power.*"

"That's good to hear," Kirk said.

"*They're fifteen minutes behind you.*"

"Understood," Kirk said.

"*I'm reversing the tractor beam that's pushing you, to slow your momentum.*"

Kirk felt the difference as soon as the engineer made the transition; a stuttering hesitation in their forward motion, then an easy glide.

"That worked. We're about to dock, Scotty," he said. "We'll keep you updated as we're able. Kirk out."

The *McRaven* loomed ahead of them, larger with every passing second. "Engines on, Mister Bunker."

"Aye, Captain. Engines on."

"Do we dare, Jim?" McCoy asked as the faint rumble of the engines came on. "We don't know how—"

"You're right, we don't," Kirk said. "But if we're going to reach the *McRaven*'s hangar deck, we need thrusters."

They were approaching the *McRaven* on its port side. As the most recent addition to the clustered mass, it was on the outside, some distance from the huge vessel in the center. To reach the hangar deck, they had to get to the rear of the ship, and hope the doors would open.

"Bring us in, Mister Bunker," Kirk said.

Bunker was already concentrating on edging the shuttle into position. "Aye."

The shuttle responded appropriately to Bunker's efforts. Kirk dared to hope that Spock had been right, and the effects of the dimensional fold were concentrated at its edges. If they had already seen the worst of it, then it would be more than possible to send other shuttles in to carry survivors back to the *Enterprise*.

If there were survivors.

There were, he knew, a lot of ifs in that plan.

Still, there was a chance.

He would take it.

The shuttle moved easily around the *McRaven*. In a few minutes, they were approaching the hangar deck, in the engineering section.

The doors were closed.

"Hail the ship," Kirk instructed.

"Shuttlecraft *Galileo Two* calling *U.S.S. McRaven*," Bunker called. "Come in, *McRaven*."

Only silence greeted them.

"Come in, *McRaven*. This is shuttlecraft *Galileo Two*, from the *U.S.S. Enterprise*."

No answer.

"Try opening the hangar doors remotely," Kirk said.

"But—"

"She's a Federation starship," Kirk pointed out. "There's no guarantee that the ship will recognize us, but there's no guarantee that it won't."

Bunker pressed some buttons on his control panel. "No response," he said.

"Are you sure?"

"Captain, I—"

"Wait for it," Kirk instructed.

"Aye, sir," Bunker said. He looked out the forward ports.

The hangar deck doors were parting.

"Damn," Bunker whispered.

"Put us down gently," Kirk told him. "Leave room for the second shuttle if you can."

"The *McRaven* still has power," Spock observed. "At least minimally."

"So it appears."

"Maybe there are people alive on her after all," McCoy said.

"Let's hope," Kirk agreed. The hangar deck was empty, but it was also depressurized, so there might have been crew in the control room.

Bunker set the shuttle down with a gentle bump. After a couple of minutes, everybody disembarked to wait for the second shuttle. The artificial gravity was still working, but the team remained in their environmental suits, phasers or tricorders in hand, depending on whether they were looking for trouble or signs of life. In such a situation, either consideration was equally valid, Kirk believed.

"Mister Gao, Ensign Romer," he said, picking two members of the security crew essentially at random, "go up and check the control room. I'd like to know if there's anybody at the switch."

"Aye, sir," Romer said. She and Gao clomped up the steps, walking heavily in their bulky suits. Kirk watched them go, then turned his attention to the view outside the bay doors. From the anomaly's inside, the view was no less strange than it had appeared from the *Enterprise*. Instead of the blackness of space, he looked out through a kind of uneven violet light, ragged at the edges, like clouds trying hard to rain. Energy pulsed through the bizarre sky in brilliant lemon streaks. He thought he could smell something reminiscent of cherries. That was impossible, though. He was imagining things. Olfactory hallucinations.

Moments later, the security team returned from

their scouting mission. "Control room's empty," Gao reported.

"Noted," Kirk said. He had expected as much. Nothing about this mission was going to be easy. He had already reached that conclusion, and circumstances appeared determined to prove him right.

Twelve

The *McRaven* was empty.

More than empty. Once they had gotten the hangar deck pressurized and had moved into the rest of the ship, they found rust coating the walls, and greenish mold as thick as Spanish moss draping from the overheads and blotching the decks. The lights were on, but dim, the artificial gravity functional, and the atmosphere breathable. They took their helmets off, but kept them close.

"This looks like it hasn't been occupied in two hundred years," Kirk said.

"Maybe it hasn't," McCoy said.

"It's not that old," Kirk said. "The *McRaven*'s only five years old. It's impossible."

"Clearly not," Spock said. "It exists."

"I'm having my doubts," McCoy muttered.

"What I meant," McCoy said, "is that we still don't know the effects of what Spock calls the dimensional fold. Maybe two hundred years in here doesn't mean the same thing as out there."

"Exactly," Spock said. He and McCoy agreeing so readily was only slightly less implausible than the condition of the abandoned vessel.

"The ship's systems seem to be workin'," McCoy added. "At minimal power, but functional. So what happened to everybody?"

"If you're right about the time differential," Kirk said, "they might have all died long ago."

"Or, depending upon the rules of the reality we currently inhabit, they might never have been here," the Vulcan observed.

"What's that supposed to mean?" McCoy demanded.

"Simply that we do not know the limitations of the dimensional fold," Spock explained. "It is possible that not just dimensions, but universes, intersect here. This *McRaven* might exist in a universe in which it never had a crew."

"You're makin' my brain hurt," McCoy said.

"That is not my intention." Once again, Kirk thought he might have seen the beginnings of a smile play across the science officer's face, a slight crinkling at the corners of the eyes.

They examined the cabin that Ambassador D'Asaro had used. Most surfaces were covered in the same rust and moist, dark fur they'd found elsewhere. Nothing indicated how long it had been since anyone had been aboard the ship. With the stuttering turbolifts, Kirk's party made it to the bridge. The minimal power aboard wasn't adequate to get the ship's main computer working, so they couldn't access that for the ship's records.

Then a scouting party led by Stanley Vandella returned to the bridge. "Captain," Vandella said. "There's
something you've got to see."

"Haven't I seen enough?" Kirk replied, in jest. He
beckoned the rest of the team. "We've learned all we're
going to in here."

Vandella led the group off the bridge, down to
the crew quarters on Deck 6. "We were checking the
various crew decks to see if we could find any sign of
recent habitation," he said. "Instead, we found—"

"Don't keep us in suspense, man," McCoy groused.
"What is it?"

"It's . . . hard to describe," Vandella said. "You'll see
in a minute."

Kirk noticed a strange odor tingeing the air in
the corridor. Without his helmet on, he could smell
the outside world again. This aroma wasn't exactly
like the one he had imagined earlier, but it was close
enough that he had to wonder if he had, in fact, really smelled something. There was an undercurrent
of cherries to it, but cherries that were spoiling, and
mixed with another odor, at once familiar and strange.
It took a while for him to realize that it was reminiscent of exhaust from Uncle Frank's farm truck.

Then Vandella stopped before a door, just one
more anonymous entry into a standard crew member's quarters. He punched the control on the outside,
and the door labored open with a wheeze.

And through the door was not crew quarters, but

an opening. Into what, Kirk was unsure. Even more uncertain was what comprised the opening. It looked organic, walls and ceiling and floor coated with thick fungus or moss, with pinkish patches beneath, glistening and wet.

The opening looked, in fact, like a throat, with a pink and green mottled uvula hanging down from the center.

"What is . . . ?" Kirk began.

"A passageway into the largest vessel," Spock said, consulting his tricorder. "This side of the saucer is the only part of the *McRaven* in direct contact with it."

"The ship that's central to the cluster of ships," Kirk said. "As if it were exerting its own gravitational pull."

"Correct."

"Jim, we oughta get out of here," McCoy said. "Nothin' good can come of hangin' around this place a minute longer."

Spock raised an eyebrow. "This is a singularly unique research opportunity, Doctor."

"It's a damn death trap!"

"It's still a rescue mission, Bones," Kirk said. "The *McRaven* is—somehow—joined to that larger ship. Which is where we detected electrical impulses that might be signs of life. We have to check it out."

McCoy shook his head slowly, as if he were in the presence of lunatics whose delusions had to be tolerated lest they become dangerous. "All right," he said. "I don't like it, but you're the captain."

Kirk turned to O'Meara, who was holding a tricorder at the ready. "Scan past that opening, Mister O'Meara. Since there's no visible barrier, the atmosphere appears to be safe to breathe, but I'd rather not take chances."

"Yes, sir," O'Meara said. He pointed the instrument at the opening, stepping across the threshold. Kirk had a sudden mental image of the throat closing with him inside it, swallowing him whole. O'Meara might have had the same thought, but he did his duty.

He looked at the tricorder's display, tapped the instrument's side gently, then gave it a serious whack.

"Something wrong?" Kirk asked.

O'Meara turned back toward the away team. "According to this, Captain, we should be engulfed in flames. This says the atmosphere is almost pure hydrogen, at ninety thousand degrees." He glanced at the display panel again. "Oh, and it says that you're all alive, but not even remotely human. Should I be worried, sir?"

"Apparently the tricorders have fallen victim to the dimensional fold's usual effect on Starfleet instrumentation," Spock observed.

Kirk took out his phaser and fired at the near wall. Nothing. The captain dialed up the phaser from stun to three-quarter power and fired again. The wall showed a scorch pattern. O'Meara flipped open his communicator. "Dead," he reported.

"It seems that the fold is affecting all of our

instruments," Kirk observed. "Reset your phasers. And keep close. We need to find out if any of the *McRaven*'s crew is alive."

"Your first assessment still stands," McCoy said. "The thing's wide open. We can stand here and breathe. Any reason to think we couldn't on the other side?"

"I'll check," Tikolo volunteered.

"Fine," Kirk said. "Careful, though."

"Yes, sir."

She raised her phaser, ready to fire, and stepped quickly through the opening. The gullet didn't contract; no giant teeth came down on her like a dentate portcullis. She stopped on the far side and faced the others. "Seems fine. A little humid, maybe, but no apparent ill effects. Gravity seems Earth-normal."

Kirk could feel the humidity leaking out to his side of the passage. "If the ship is open to the *McRaven* and the atmosphere is breathable, we leave our environmental suits here," he said. "I'm feeling a little cramped in mine."

He started to peel it off. Doctor McCoy looked for a second as if he wanted to object, then shrugged and did the same. When everybody was down to their standard duty uniforms, Kirk said, "Let's find out what's inside this thing."

He stepped through the throat. Spock followed, then the rest. "Mister Spock," Kirk said, "can you explain this somewhat atypical docking procedure?"

"I cannot, Captain."

"Care to venture a guess?"

"I have no . . . valid hypothesis."

"Well, I don't believe it," McCoy said, his tone betraying his amazement.

"What, Bones?"

"Something has finally struck him speechless! I was beginning to think it'd never happen."

"I am far from speechless, Doctor," Spock objected. "Unlike some, I simply choose not to fabricate answers when I am unable to provide accurate ones."

McCoy started to let the remark slide, then thought better of it. "Jim, I think he just called me a liar."

Kirk shrugged. Spock replied, "I did no such thing."

"Come on," Kirk said. "Let's try to find this monstrous ship's bridge."

The ship was like no vessel Kirk had ever seen. It appeared almost ancient in design, like something Jules Verne might have conceived. It had exposed conduit and piping for electrical, plumbing, and environmental systems, doors with heavy, complex latching systems that took considerable effort to open or close, and corridor ceilings, walls, and floors made of some raw metal, without ornament or decoration. Ladders, not turbolifts, joined the various decks. Except for the fact that such an enormous vessel had been capable, apparently, of interstellar travel, it looked like some-body's first attempt at space flight.

Of course, if there had been any more elaborate touches, they were hidden beneath the layers of muck and mold and dripping, glistening scum that coated nearly every surface, as if the ship had been submerged in a swamp for a century or two. It even smelled swampy, with the fetid, rank air of decaying life. The tricorders had denied that the stuff that looked so moldy was organic in nature, but Kirk didn't know what else it might be. Then again, the tricorders couldn't be trusted.

The scale and placement of most things hinted at essentially humanoid construction. Acting on the assumption that humans and human-type beings tended to put controls in elevated places, they worked their way up ladders (some rungs, decayed by age and rust, giving out beneath their weight) in search of the ship's bridge. Dim light glowed from what looked like flat cross sections of some luminescent stone mounted on the walls, providing just enough illumination to find their way around.

The higher they climbed, the grander the corridors became. They were wider up here, the doors more elaborately constructed. The walls were still slicked with muck, and any paint or other decorative touches had long since been stripped away, but Kirk had the sense that there was a distinct class system at work, and the higher decks had been the territory of the upper classes. It was empty, all of it, but Kirk couldn't shake the feeling that it had not been so for long, despite appearances. A long-vacant house felt different than one occupied but empty at the moment. The same applied to starships, he thought, and this one seemed to him as if its occupants had merely stepped out, only minutes—or a century—before.

"Captain," O'Meara said as Kirk paused before yet another ladder between decks. "The tricorder's working again."

Spock checked his own. "Indeed. The atmosphere is comparable to that inside the *McRaven*. We are not being slowly poisoned."

"Good to know," Kirk said. "If they're right this time."

"Still no signs of life, outside our own party," O'Meara reported. "But I am once again picking up those electrical impulses. They're all around us."

"A ship of ghosts," Kirk said softly.

"What's that, Jim?" McCoy asked.

"Oh, nothing, Bones. Nothing. Let's see what's upstairs."

Thirteen

They came early in the morning, out of the rising sun. Aleshia heard the noise from her bed. She stumbled past the snoring form of her father and out of the house. Down the hill, she saw that others had emerged from their homes as well. Everyone looked toward the east, shielding their eyes with their hands and blinking against the brightness. She did the same.

She saw only vague shapes, at first, their outlines indistinct against the sun's brilliant orb. As they grew closer, they became more solid. First it appeared to be just one, then that one differentiated into several, then many. They might have been birds, an enormous flock of them, soaring in on outstretched wings, but for the buzz they made. When Aleshia had first heard it, the noise was unfamiliar, metallic and grating. As she stood watching them come ever closer, the noise magnified, intensified to the point that her teeth ached, then her bones. The earth beneath her feet was vibrating. She heard a pattering noise behind her; turning, she saw dust shaken from the eaves of her home and cascading to the ground. The morning air smelled brittle, somehow.

Father came outside, then, his pants unbuttoned, his shirt thrown on haphazardly. Whiskers sprouted from his chin and cheeks like the first shoots of grass coaxed from once-frozen earth by early spring rains. He blinked at the sunlight. "What is it?" he grumbled.

"I don't know, Father, look!"

"I asked you so I wouldn't have to look for myself, idiot!" She half expected a cuff, but she had gone too far from the door. He'd have to take several steps to reach her, and that appeared to be beyond his ability at the moment. Unsteadily, he reached for the doorjamb, then leaned back against it. "Noisy, though."

"Yes," Aleshia said. Already, the sound of the approaching . . . whatever they were, was loud enough to drown out normal conversation. She raised her voice. "Yes!" she said again. "They are noisy!"

Father cast a dismissive glance at the approaching objects, then went back inside, slamming the door behind him. *As if,* Aleshia thought, *mere doors and walls and windows could hold at bay such a din.*

Some of the objects—not birds, she could see now; their wings were far too rigid, and they would have been many times larger than any bird she had ever seen—dropped suddenly, plummeting toward the ground. Others kept their altitude.

Kistral pointed toward the ones sailing to earth. "They're landing!" he said. "It's them, I know it is!"

He didn't have to define what he meant by *them*. Everyone knew.

The ones who stay away.

They had, for as long as anyone could remember, purchased any excess crops the villagers raised, and livestock, too. They never came in person, but sent wagons that rumbled fiercely and belched smoke and were drawn by no animals at all. In those wagons were folk from the cities of the Eastern Belt. The people were different each time; Aleshia could only remember seeing a familiar face once, and on his second trip, the young man stayed inside the wagon and let the other, the newcomer, do the talking.

Everybody knew the crops weren't meant for those cities, though legend had it that once those glittering places were the village's only customers. The men and women who came with the wagons made no secret of it. They had enough to eat, if only just. No, the crops were hauled away toward the cities, and somewhere along the way they were picked up by the ones who stay away, those who never deigned to show their faces in the villages.

Aleshia had gone to see Margyan, just a fortnight earlier. It had taken time to steel herself, to drum up the courage to walk into that house's front courtyard, with its dry fountain and paving stones shattered by the things thrown at Margyan over the years. She was almost universally reviled; stories about her had pet-rified Aleshia since childhood. But when Aleshia had made herself knock, oh so timidly, on the wooden door, Margyan had opened it almost at once. The crone's face Aleshia saw occasionally at market or in the road, a mass of wrinkles and graying skin under-neath her hood, seemed transformed in the daylight. Margyan wore no hood; she was smiling broadly and her smile smoothed the wrinkles, and late after-noon sunlight erased the gray and gave her flesh a warm glow. Her hair was mostly white with patches of silver, reminding Aleshia of snow flurries in the hills. "Come in, come in," Margyan had said. "You're Aleshia, yes?"

"I am, yes," Aleshia had replied. Her knees, she re-membered, would not stop trembling, threatening to dump her into the dirt outside Margyan's home. The old woman had invited her in, and made her com-fortable in the nicest, softest chair Aleshia had ever felt. She almost sank into it, as if she were sitting on a cloud. Margyan brought her tea, surprisingly sweet and fruity, and made pleasant conversation until she was sitting opposite Aleshia, each with her own sim-mering mug.

"Your father," Margyan said then. Her smile van-ished. "He beats you, yes? He's a worthless lout, that one."

"No, he's—" Something in Margyan's expression made her halt the lie, untold. "Yes," she said. "He does beat me. And he won't do a lick of work."

"Worthless," Margyan said again. "But I'm sorry, you came for something in particular, not just to be enthralled by my insights and worldly ways."

Aleshia's voice seemed to leave her. She opened her mouth and a squeak emerged, a sound a stepped-on baby toad might make. She cleared her throat and tried again. "My friend Gillayne," she managed. "She says you know about the ones who stay away. She says they're really the giants, and the ones who sent the burning rains."

"Ahh," Margyan said. She rose from her chair and drew the curtain, plunging the room into twilight. "Are you sure you want to know?"

"I am," Aleshia said. "I'm sure. I must know."

"Once you've learned it, you can't unlearn it," Margyan warned. "You won't be able to forget."

Aleshia bunched her skirts in her fists and pounded on her own thighs. "I don't care! I want to know the truth!"

"If you insist," Margyan said. "But always remember that I tried to discourage you. Curiosity is part of life, the sign of a superior intellect. But it has a way of demanding its own price, later on. When the time comes and the payment's due, I don't want you thinking ill of poor old Margyan"

"Never!"

Margyan chuckled. "That's as big as lie as I've heard all year," she said. "But no matter. You want the truth, yes? Here it is. . . ."

• • •

Aleshia remembered that conversation as she watched the objects hurtling toward them. Kistral was right, they were landing. When they neared the ground, enormous clouds of dust billowed into the air, and when they actually came to rest, the racket was even worse than before. A roar like that of a hundred wagons seemed to emanate from each one, joined by clanking, mechanical sounds almost buried under the roar, and the grinding noise as they scraped over sand and rock and field.

By that time everyone in the village, or everyone who could walk or hobble or crawl outside, had come to watch. The more people crowded together, the more Aleshia heard theories and rumors about their visitors. "Monsters," someone said. "They're not *inside* those things," another warned. "They *are* those things, with skin of steel and sharp-edged wings!" One man started blubbering. "They've come for our children," he said between sobs. "Our livestock's no longer good enough."

Margyan had opened Aleshia's eyes, though. She looked at the villagers gathered there, fewer than half of what there would have been, not even a year earlier. A third, more like. She gathered her skirts and stepped down the slope to Gillayne's side. "That's not them," she said quietly. "They are inside, and they're going to come out. And they aren't here for the children, but for all of us."

Gillayne eyed her with surprise. "You've been to see Margyan?"

"I meant to tell you, but I haven't had the chance. I've been so busy."

"Some of us have a welcoming gift for them," Gillayne said. She drew Aleshia's gaze down with her eyes, until Aleshia saw what she held beneath her own skirts: a hatchet, its edge sharpened until it gleamed with wicked purpose. "Had I known you knew, I'd have told you sooner."

"Who else?" Aleshia asked. Her heart had started to flutter; she did not want to believe Margyan's suspicions, but worse still was the idea that her friends might act upon them.

Gillayne made a point of not looking at anyone she named. "Kistral, Claen, Nakya, Virong. Some others."

Aleshia looked at the number of objects—she didn't know what to call them; flying wagons?—that had landed, and were even now sitting motionless as the dust clouds settled around them. They were big, she realized, far larger than the biggest wagon she had ever seen. Each could hold dozens of people, easily. Hundreds, perhaps.

"That's suicide," she said. "You can't fight that."

"That's what they want us to believe," Gillayne countered. "Suicide or not, I don't go down without trying."

"What about me?" Aleshia asked. "I have no weapon."

"It's not too late. Get an ax or a bow or a knife from your house. A hammer. Anything."

Aleshia glanced up the hill. Father stood by the door, hand inside his shirt, scratching his belly. His face was dull and mean. If that was what life had to offer, the chance to marry someone like that, to raise children who would become that in their turn . . .

"No," she said aloud.

"What?"

"I won't accept that there's nothing else, nothing beyond what we've got here. I know there's more this world can offer."

"You'd best hurry, if you hope to ever find out."

"Right back," she said. As she started up the hill, the flying wagons opened and people came out. They looked much like the villagers, just people after all, but their clothing was like nothing she had ever seen, and their weapons even less so.

Sixty or seventy of them emerged from the insides of the flying things, and they came toward the village. As they approached, one of them called out in an accent that was strange but understandable. "We aren't here to hurt you," she said. "You must come with us now. It's time."

Yignay strutted to the front of the pack of villagers. "Come with you where? In those things?"

"Just do as you're told, old man," the woman said. "Don't make trouble."

"This place is our home," Yignay argued.

"Used to be, you mean."

Aleshia reached her house. Her father shot her a vicious glare, as if the whole affair were somehow her fault, but he stepped aside and let her pass. She went to the kitchen and found the biggest knife they owned, with a blade she kept keen by scraping it on the sharpening stone every second new moon. She made no attempt to hide it, but ran from the house with it clutched in her fist.

She was just in time to see Yignay scoop a stone from the ground. It was smaller than his fist, but not by much. "Always *has* been, I mean," he said. "Always *will* be."

The woman had come several steps closer, but she was still well outside the distance that Yignay could hurl a stone. The rest came right behind her, bunched up together, carrying objects Aleshia could no more name than she could the things they wore. "Don't," the woman said.

Yignay threw the rock.

The woman pressed something on the thing she carried. Purple light burst from the end of it and struck Yignay. He cried out and threw his arms to his side, and Aleshia could see blood spray from his chest and land on the ground around him with a sound like a sudden rain shower. He fell to his knees and kept falling, pitching forward onto his ruined chest.

The aroma of burned flesh wafted up the hill to Aleshia, and she realized her mouth was watering despite her horror. She had not realized how hungry she was. She swallowed it and clenched her fists until her nails dug into her palms.

Other villagers were screaming, some weeping. The woman had to raise her voice to be heard. "It doesn't have to be like that," she said. "We haven't come to fight. It's just time for you to go."

"Go where?" someone asked.

"You'll be told en route."

"We don't go until we know where, and why, and we're given time to gather our possessions," Kistral said. "What authority have you to demand anything of us?"

The woman hoisted her purple light machine. "All the authority we need. Come on, we haven't got all the time in the world."

At that, one of the other newcomers broke into laughter. "Or maybe we do," he said. "Maybe we do, at that."

Kistral charged then, lifting a lead pipe from the ground by his feet and waving it menacingly as he ran toward them. Another of the party made a purple ray hit him, and his head exploded in a mist of blood and flesh.

Tears stung Aleshia's eyes. She saw Gillayne drop the hatchet, and Nakya toss aside a bow and four arrows. Aleshia's fingers relaxed on the knife, as if it had become too hot to hold. "Put that down," her father murmured. "Save yourself, anyway." He brushed past her and lifted a shovel from behind the house. "It ain't much, against those," he said as he started down the hill, shovel held in front of his chest. "But it's all I got."

He was most of the way down the hill before one of the newcomers trained a purple light on him.

As his body tumbled down the slope, the woman at the front spoke up again. "We don't want to hurt anybody," she said. "We've just come to collect you. You're going on a little trip. You might even find it fun."

"Fun?" Margyan echoed. "Not likely."

"No!" Aleshia cried. "Not you, Margyan!"

"We've little choice, girl," Margyan replied. "Die now or go along with them. I know my druthers."

"But—"

Margyan couldn't hear Aleshia's objection, though; she drowned it out with her own ululating cry as she rushed toward those who had once stayed away, but did no longer, and then her screams as the purple light took her, too, and the handful who tried to join her.

When that died down, it was quiet. Tears rolled down Aleshia's cheeks, and most others' that she saw, as she and the other villagers allowed themselves to be herded, like so much livestock, toward the flying wagons. She took Gillayne's hand in hers, looked back at her house one last time, realized that although there were many things she would miss, that wasn't one of them. Could wherever they would be taken be any worse than home? She stepped up a ramp into the flying wagon's sleek interior.

It was like nothing she had ever imagined.

Fourteen

At the top of the next ladder the *Enterprise* crew found another, wider corridor, with arched passageways instead of closed doors leading to spaces that contained all manner of instrumentation. The length of the corridor seemed endless; Kirk thought he could see it curving downward, like the curvature of the Earth, then thought briefly that it was an optical illusion, an impossibility. Then he reminded himself where he was, and that what was impossible in other places was commonplace here. So maybe he did see the ship reach a distant horizon and dip away, and maybe it cycled back beyond that point and continued on. The thing seemed to stretch practically forever.

"Fascinating," Spock muttered, breaking Kirk's reverie.

"What is?"

"This seems to be the bridge," Spock said. "We are used to a ship's bridge being a confined space where the command crew can communicate and access the instrumentation necessary to pilot the vessel."

"That is the definition of a bridge, more or less," Kirk said.

"And yet, here are instrument clusters that, upon brief inspection, appear to fulfill those functions."

"You can tell what these gadgets do?" McCoy asked.

"Not precisely, no. There is writing on some of them, which I believe to be Ixtoldan."

"Ixtoldan?" Kirk echoed. "Really?"

"Again, I am not certain, but I think it is. I have been studying Ixtoldan culture and history en route. There are other, similar written languages, and I do not read Ixtoldan, but it looks Ixtoldan to me."

"Fascinating."

"Indeed. Perhaps more so because none of the Ixtoldan histories mention a ship like this. Interstellar travel is relatively new to them, and this ship appears to be ancient."

"Excuse me, Mister Spock," Ensign Bunker said. "Couldn't that be an effect of what you called the dimensional folding?"

"It could indeed. But even if the apparent age of the ship were disguised by that, the very existence of such an enormous ship, obviously intended to carry a huge passenger load, considerable cargo, or both, should have been reported somewhere. I have seen no reference to it in any history of their space program."

"So we're on a ship that might be Ixtoldan," Kirk said, "which we found while traveling to Ixtolde, carrying a delegation of Ixtoldan diplomats, none of whom wanted us to explore this ship. Curiouser and curiouser."

"It's more than just curious," McCoy said. "It's damn fishy, if you ask me."

"Especially," Kirk said, "if you add the fact that one of the ships connected to it was carrying our ambassador-to-be to Ixtolde."

"What do you make of it, Captain?" a security team member named Aldous Beachwood asked. He had strawberry blond hair, clear gray eyes, and a disarmingly gentle manner. Kirk had seen him in action, and he knew that the gentleness went away fast under the right circumstances.

"I'm not at all sure yet," Kirk said. "But I recommend that we maintain our vigilance. Something doesn't add up about all of this." He eyed the instruments around them, the control panels that followed no pattern he could discern. "What's your take on the ship's controls, Mister Spock? Does the scattered nature of them mean anything to you?"

"Crew communication was performed in some fashion other than verbal," Spock said. "Or, if verbal, then through electronic means. Possibly through telepathic means; I see nothing that appears to be a microphone or a speaker, although it is possible that those were attached via cables that have been removed or deteriorated in place."

"So you're just guessing," McCoy said.

"I am engaging in informed speculation, yes." He

stepped over to an instrument cluster, studied it up close for a few moments, then turned back toward the others. He took two steps, then seemed to be jostled aside. "Excuse me," he said. He looked toward where whatever he had bumped into would have been, but there was nothing there. When he faced Kirk again, he looked puzzled.

"Something wrong?" Kirk asked.

"I was certain that I ran into someone," Spock replied. "I saw no one as I approached, but I distinctly felt a solid object touch my shoulder. So I apologized, believing that I had not seen somebody."

"There's nobody there."

"Indeed."

"You bumped into empty air?" McCoy said. "That's rich. I could do some informed speculatin' about that."

"No," Spock corrected. "I did not bump into empty air. I bumped into something presently unseen. I encountered something."

"It's this ship," Bunker said anxiously. "There's something wrong with it. Captain, I think we ought to get out of here."

"In due time, Mister Bunker."

"Yes, sir." He was gripping his phaser so tightly that his knuckles had gone white.

Kirk stepped past where Spock had been, bracing himself for a physical encounter with an invisible object. It didn't happen, and he reached the instrument panel without incident. Above it was a viewport looking out toward the jumble of ships surrounding the possibly Ixtoldan vessel. He was swiveling away from the port when the ship gave a sudden jerk, like an aircraft flying in atmosphere encountering the wake of another, or an air pocket. He caught himself on the instrument console; others threw out their arms to brace themselves or spread their feet wider. A few of the crew members chuckled nervously.

"That was interesting," McCoy said. "Felt like we were rammed."

Kirk looked out the viewport again, in case any of the ships outside had shifted position and collided with the big one.

Nothing had changed, that he could determine.

But reflected in the glass—as if standing right behind him—he saw something else that startled him, making him spin around.

"Jim?" McCoy said. "What is it?"

Nobody there but the landing party. Kirk shook his head. "Nothing, Bones. My mistake."

"You look like you've seen a ghost, man. You're white as a sheet."

"Maybe I have." He looked out the viewport again, only not out, but in: at the reflection of the corridor behind him, which Spock had identified as one large, spread-out bridge.

And there he was again. Uncle Frank, standing over Kirk's left shoulder. His cheeks were stubbled with the growth of several days, his eyes half-hooded from a lifetime spent squinting against the sun, his mouth set in a grimly determined line. Just the way Kirk had known him. Even his smell was there, that particular combination of sweat, horse, and campfire that Kirk had always associated with the man. He could almost hear his name, "*Jim*my-boy," floating in the air like something somebody had said, realized only in retrospect.

But that had been decades ago. Uncle Frank had died since then. And during his lifetime, he had never left Earth.

Another impossibility. Uncle Frank wasn't here, couldn't be here. It was nothing but a figment, a hallucination brought on by—what? By the unknown, maybe unknowable nature of the anomaly? Or something else?

McCoy would press him on it, would ask him what he had seen, try to psychoanalyze him on the spot. He didn't want that. At this moment, Kirk wanted the same thing Bunker did—to get the hell off this ship and back to the *Enterprise*. There was nobody left here. The ambassador was dead, as was the *McRaven*'s crew. He started trying to compose a story for Bones, something that would deter him from pushing for more.

But even as he faced the doctor, opening his mouth to spin some sort of nonsense, the ship jolted once again, and emergency klaxons began to sound.

Was this yet another example of the impossible?

The ship's systems didn't appear to be operational, or only barely so. The artificial gravity was fully functional, lighting was minimal, the *Enterprise* crew could survive in the environment. But the emergency alert system seemed, by all deafening indications, to be performing at full capacity.

"What in the hell?" McCoy asked.

"I don't know," Kirk said. "But I—"

A shout cut him off, loud enough to be heard despite the ongoing blare of the klaxons, and seemingly fraught with emotion, with anguish. It was Bunker, and when Kirk spotted him, he was racing toward a corner—a corner Kirk didn't remember seeing before—phaser in his hand. "Come back!" Bunker cried.

"Bunker, wait!" Kirk called out.

Bunker ignored him and vanished around the corner.

"Who's he chasing?" Kirk asked of no one in particular.

"I didn't see anyone, sir," Tikolo said. "I was right next to him. Anything he saw, I would have seen, but I didn't."

Kirk did a quick head count. Bunker was the only one of their party missing. "All right," he said. He pointed to four other members of the security team. "You go with Tikolo. Bring Bunker back. Petty Officer Tikolo, you're in charge."

"Yes, sir," Tikolo said. She and the other four raced off, around the corner and out of sight.

And in their wake, Kirk hoped that this somewhat unorthodox rescue mission had not just become a major disaster.

"They'll be fine, Jim," McCoy said. He didn't sound convinced, much less convincing. The klaxons had stopped, so that was a relief. "And I'm not sure there's anything this damn ship can throw at Miranda Tikolo that she hasn't already seen."

"You're right, Bones. I just hate to split up."

"I understand. Now, before you stall me again, what did you see out that port?"

Kirk gave McCoy and Spock a barely perceptible nod, and both men stepped closer to him. "I saw my uncle Frank," he said quietly. "He was standing right behind me, as surely as you're in front of me."

"He is dead, Captain. And has been, for many years."

"I know that, Spock. Of course he is. It was an optical illusion, a—"

"A figment of your imagination?" McCoy finished for him. "Like whatever Bunker's chasing?"

"It's this ship," Kirk said. "It's playing tricks on us."

"We can get off it any time."

"Can we access its memory banks, Spock? Try to find out what happened to everybody?"

"This ship has less available power than the *McRaven*," Spock replied. "Enough to power very basic systems, but nothing complicated. I do not believe we would be able to power the memory banks, if we could even determine how they work, and I do not believe that even if we could do that, we would understand what they showed us."

"So we may never know what happened here," Kirk said.

"There are some mysteries that will never be solved," McCoy said. "Anyway, what fun would the universe be if every question had an answer?"

Spock stared at Bones, a quizzical look on his face. "What?" McCoy asked.

"I do not understand your question."

"It was rhetorical," McCoy said. "You understand rhetorical, don't you?"

"I do."

"Do you understand this? Go jump in a lake."

"If there were a lake present, I would understand it literally," Spock said. "Since there is not, I understand it rhetorically. And—"

"And what?"

"And, Doctor McCoy, I believe the correct response is, the same to you."

Bones appeared to be composing a retort, but before he had a chance to deliver it, the ship was shaken by another powerful jolt. "What in the blazes is going on here?" he demanded.

"We've landed!" Ensign Romer cried. She was standing near one of the round viewports installed above the instrument panels. "Look! I know this place!"

Kirk stepped back to the port he had just used.

They had not been close to any planets at that point, only moments before. Then again, Uncle Frank had not really been standing behind him, so any evidence provided by his eyes was not to be trusted.

They appeared to have touched down on a planetary surface. A green-tinged light washed over a rugged, boulder-strewn landscape, barren of life. The landing spot was in a valley, ringed by jagged cliffs. "Where is it, Ensign?" he asked.

"It looks like an asteroid I visited during my first posting after the Academy," she said. "It had a number, not a name."

"And was it close by?"

"Well . . . no, now that you mention it. But . . ."

"Yes?"

"But, weren't we told that the normal rules of time and space don't necessarily apply here?"

"That's right."

"So just about anything's possible, isn't it?"

Kirk glanced at the view outside again. "Possible, yes. But likely?"

Romer was right; no possibility could be entirely discounted. But the more reasonable explanation—if reason counted for anything within the fold—was that they were being deceived, the same way Kirk had been when he saw his uncle. He didn't know precisely how to explain it: mass hallucination? Mirage? Something more complicated, maybe even sinister? Without more investigation, he couldn't begin to say.

"I guess not," Romer replied. She sounded wistful. "It's strange, though. The asteroid always seemed like a special place to me. The first place I actually walked on the surface of something that wasn't Earth. I was in love, I was full of wonder and thrilled to be part of Starfleet. I've been thinking about it, lately, and now . . . it's like I could step outside and be back there."

"I do not recommend it," Spock said.

Romer released a dry chuckle. "No, I suppose not."

Kirk looked toward the doorway through which Bunker had disappeared. Still no sign of Tikolo and her party, either. He flipped open his communicator and tried to raise her, without success.

"We've been here too long already," he declared. "Let's find them. Everybody stick together, and don't trust anything you see." Remembering Spock's apparent encounter with the invisible, he added, "Whether you see it or not."

Fifteen

Montgomery Scott figured that, whatever the away team was facing, by being left behind he had gotten the raw end of the deal. Of course he had to remain on board the *Enterprise*. That was the chief engineer's duty, after all. But no evil alien threat, he was certain, could possibly be as utterly terrifying as a bridge full of bureaucrats. And with the captain, Mister Spock, and Doctor McCoy gone, he was the one who had to deal with them.

Or die trying.

"Surely you understand, Mister Scott," the one named Gonzales was saying. Or was it Rinaldo? They all ran together in his head, combining to form almost an entire human being. "In high-level diplomacy, actions speak louder than words. Words are also important, of course. But we can tell the Ixtoldans, until we're blue in the face, that their petition to join the Federation is important to us, that we take it seriously, and that we would very much like to include them in the community of civilized worlds. If our deeds fail to match our rhetoric, though, then our words might as well be meaningless babble."

You said it, Scotty thought, *not I.* He managed not to say it, instead blurting out, "It isn't like we're sittin' here enjoyin' the view! There's a reason the captain went to that ship!"

"There might have been," the diplomat said. Gonzales, he was sure this one was Gonzales. "But by this time, that reason would seem to be moot."

"You think we're just gonna take off without our captain and the landing party?"

"Of course not," Gonzales replied. "But they could be recalled to the ship and we might still be able to meet our commitments."

"So you missed the part where we canna reach them?"

"They will report in at some point, will they not? When they do, you need to tell them to return immediately to the *Enterprise*."

"*If* they report in, I'll not be takin' orders from you!"

"Mister Scott," another one said. This was Perkins, he knew that. "Mister Scott, Mister Gonzales is, most assuredly, not trying to command you to do anything. He's merely suggesting the most reasonable course of action to achieve our mutual goals."

"You must've learned a different definition for 'mutual' than I did. My goal is to keep the *Enterprise* steady while we wait for the away team to finish what they're doin'. Which, as I recall, is lookin' for one of *your* people." He remembered too late that the presence of the ambassador aboard the *McRaven* had been a secret, one the *Enterprise* officers were not supposed to know. To their professional credit, none of the diplomats allowed their surprise to show.

"We are, of course, concerned about Mister D'Asaro," Rinaldo said. She sounded just like the others, as if they'd gone to pretentiousness school together. "Deeply, deeply concerned. But all available evidence seems to indicate that we're too late to help Mister D'Asaro, or anyone else with the misfortune to have been aboard the *McRaven*. Given that fact, the wisest course would be to do as Mister Gonzales suggests and make all due haste toward Ixtolde."

"Precisely," Chan'ya said. She and her retinue had also crowded onto the bridge. When Scotty had watched them emerge from the turbolift, he knew at once that they had orchestrated the moment, trying to intimidate him with their numbers. Having failed to dissuade the captain, they thought they could bulldoze the obviously more pliant chief engineer. "The fact that there are no life-forms aboard the *McRaven* has been determined. Rather than waste more time with a search-and-rescue mission when there is no one to rescue, surely the armaments on this ship and our own have the capability to destroy the *McRaven* and the ship she appears to be linked with. Then we could continue to our planet."

"With all due respect," Scotty said, "I dinna see any reason to destroy the ships, whether they're empty or not. That would be a waste of our resources and yours. If we're leavin', why not just leave?"

"The ships seem to have some sort of gravitational pull," Chan'ya replied. "Particularly that larger one. Their destruction would help other vessels resist that pull, and therefore the dimensional anomaly, would it not?"

"It might, at that," Scotty had to admit. "But so would warnin' buoys telling ships to avoid the vicinity."

"The captain and his team," Chan'ya said. "They remain on the *McRaven*, no?"

"The anomaly disrupts our instrumentation," Scotty said. "So we canna be sure where they are."

"If they went onto the other ship, that would surely be reason enough to recall them?"

Scotty turned from the Ixtoldans to the Federation diplomats, finding no help there. He glanced at the rest of the bridge crew. Chekov was busying himself with instruments, Sulu watching in what looked like frank amazement. A ghost of a smile illuminated Uhura's face. "How many times can I say it? We canna reach them at the moment! They'll try to get in touch when they can, and we're still tryin' to get to them— we were, that is, until you lot came in and distracted us. When they're ready, they'll signal us and we'll fetch them back."

Minister Chan'ya stared at him as if she were trying to read his mind. As far as he knew, she might have been—he had no idea what sorts of telepathic abilities Ixtoldans might possess. None had been admitted to, that he knew of, but that didn't mean they didn't exist. "Something else?" he asked after a while.

Chan'ya's golden skin had reddened to a deep rose. She said simply, "Well and good," then pressed her hands to her sides and swept toward the turbolift. The other Ixtoldans followed, though the Federation diplomats stayed behind. They'd plotted to arrive together; Scotty had hoped they would leave together, too. He liked dealing with engines, with machines. They had parts that fit together and worked in concert, parts that made sense. Sentient beings were something else altogether—that *sentient* thing, he guessed.

"You've insulted her," Gonzales said, leaning in close to Scotty's face.

"Me?"

"You."

"How?"

"The very fact that you don't know makes it clear that you belong in an engine room."

At that, Sulu came out of his chair. "That's enough!" he said. "We have been trying our best to perform the mission and to meet your needs, but there's no reason to be insulting. I pride myself on patience, but you, sir, have pushed that to the breaking point."

It took a lot, Scotty knew, to fray Hikaru Sulu's

nerves. Gonzales stepped back from his tirade, his eyes going wide, brows arching high. "Lieutenant," he said. "I'm afraid that all our tempers are fraying." He addressed Scotty again, offering the slightest dipping of his shoulders that could possibly be considered a bow. "My apologies, sir."

Before Scotty could respond—before he could begin to formulate an appropriate response—Gonzales and his colleagues hurried to the turbolift.

Scotty was not sorry to see them go. He only wished he had time to rig the turbolift so they couldn't return.

Bunker raced down one deck after another. When he hit a ladder he dropped down, skating along the edges instead of using the rungs. Tikolo heard his footfalls as he hurtled down a corridor, one deck below.

She reached the ladder and spun around, sliding down the way Bunker had. She hit hard, flexing her knees to absorb the impact, released the ladder, and took off in the direction she'd heard Bunker running. She heard the rest of her team hit the deck and follow, but she was already wheeling around a bend.

"Bunker!" she cried. He wasn't so far ahead that he couldn't hear her. "Bunker, it's me, Miranda! Come back!"

A door slammed. She glanced over her shoulder, saw her people taking the curve. Vandella was in front. He would be. He'd want to keep an eye on her. He seemed to be stuck on the idea that she needed to be rescued, somehow, needed a man—him, in particular—to protect her. She had tried to tell him that she'd already faced the worst, that whatever else came at her in her life could never be as terrifying.

So far, he showed no sign of understanding.

Tikolo darted through the doorway that Bunker must have taken. The hallway on the other side was narrower than the main one. At the end of a short stretch it took an abrupt turn; she couldn't tell how long it was beyond that. Thick pipes ran along one wall, close to the floor and near the ceiling. Built into the other wall were a series of steel doors that looked like lockers of some kind.

She paused long enough to let out a bellow. "Bunker!"

No response came, just the ever more distant patter of running feet.

What was he chasing? She had no clue, had not seen or heard anything, even the couple of times she had caught a faraway glimpse of him. Whatever it was had led them a dozen decks down so far. She hoped they could find their way back when the time came, but the farther they went, the less certain she was of that.

"Miranda!"

Vandella's face was flushed, sweat popping out on his brow and upper lip. "Is he down there?"

"He came this way. I can't hear anything now."

The rest of the team caught up. Tikolo didn't mind the opportunity to catch her breath, but she doubted that Bunker was availing himself of the same.

"Come on," she said urgently. Break time was over. "He's getting away from us."

"Careful, though," Eve Chandler said. "No telling what's back there." She was tall, with shoulders as broad as those of any man. Her hair was blond and cropped short, her face pleasant and open, with lovely green eyes. She was a natural leader; Tikolo wasn't sure why the captain had given command of the team to her instead of to Chandler, since she would have made the opposite choice.

Cesar Ruiz and Jamal Greene, two men she hardly knew, filled out the small squad. Greene had a tight, compact build and always made her think of a coiled spring about to release, while Ruiz was huge, with thighs almost as big around as her waist, upper arms that strained the sleeves of his uniform, and a blunt face that seemed to be all forehead and chin. Everyone had phasers drawn, since they didn't know what Bunker was chasing, or what might lurk behind any doorway or unseen corner of this strange vessel.

"I keep thinking he'll run out of ship," Tikolo said.

"It's a very substantial spacecraft," Vandella said. "If that's your plan, we could be here a long time."

"My plan, Stanley, is that he'll realize we're his friends and he'll come back."

"He'd better do it soon," Ruiz said. "Captain'll be getting worried about us."

"I've tried to reach the captain on my communicator," Tikolo said. "Bunker, too. No luck, though."

"Nothing works in this place," Greene said. "I hope the phasers still do, if we need 'em."

Tikolo pointed hers, a type-2 with a pistol grip, at an empty stretch of wall, where the corridor turned a corner, and squeezed the trigger button. A bright beam burst from it and hit the wall, where it exploded in a shower of sparks and a cloud of dark smoke. A bitter aroma filled the air. "Works," she said.

"You might have given us some warning, Miranda," Vandella said.

"Figured you'd know when I pointed the sucker what I was gonna do." She twitched her head toward the corner. "Come on, let's find Bunker and get out of here."

"Best idea I've heard all day," Greene said. "Let's do it."

Tikolo led the group around the corner, and then the next one. The corridor was unbroken, except for those locker-like doors, and when she tried a few of those, they didn't open—locked or rusted shut, or both.

But when they reached the third corner, they found only a blank wall. They fanned out, checked it for gaps or some sort of release.

"It appears to be solid," Vandella said.

"So it does," Ruiz agreed.

"I guess he didn't go this way," Tikolo said. "I was sure he did."

"If the instruments worked . . ." Greene began.

"Yeah, but they don't. At least, not with any consistency."

"Where to now, Tikolo?" Chandler asked.

Tikolo jerked her thumb over her shoulder. "Back where we came from. See if we can find him some other way."

Chandler gave an abrupt nod. Tikolo sensed disapproval flowing off her in waves. She shared Tikolo's belief that she should have been put in command. She would never say it, never question the captain's directive out loud, but her meaning was clear enough.

Tikolo shrugged it off. Captain Kirk had picked her, and that's the way it would be. She led them back down the hall, through the archway, and—

And they were no longer in the alien starship, but in a hallway she recognized, though it had been years since she'd been there.

A hallway at Starfleet Academy.

Sixteen

Kirk was the first to step off the bridge, following the route that Bunker, then the search party, had taken. He didn't know where the doorway led, but given their experience so far, he expected that the destination would not be exactly whatever he expected.

It was, in fact, not even remotely what he expected.

He found himself suddenly immersed in a cloud of greenish smoke or fog, cool and damp but with an edge that made his skin prickle. Glancing over his shoulder, he saw that the rest of the group was similarly engulfed. "Mister Spock?"

"It does not appear to be a toxic gas," Spock said. "Not that our tricorders can be relied upon."

"But if it was fast-acting," McCoy added, "we'd be feelin' it already."

"That's reassuring," Kirk said. He stepped up his pace, figuring that the sooner he was out of the cloud, the better he'd like it. Others in the party were complaining and asking questions to which there were no easy answers. Those were typically the kinds of questions that made their way to a starship captain, he knew. The easy questions could be answered by anyone. The impossible ones landed on his desk. Sometimes he surprised himself by coming up with answers, but he had a feeling that would not be the case as long as they were inside the dimensional fold.

With no more warning than when it had appeared, the cloud dissipated. But now, instead of being aboard the big alien ship, Kirk was standing on that green-tinged landscape he had seen from the ship's bridge. The ground was hard and uneven beneath his feet. A light, warm breeze wafted across him, scented with what seemed to be kiwi and nutmeg and maybe a hint of gunpowder. He could understand why Romer had liked the place, if what he was experiencing was at all indicative of the actuality.

"This really isn't possible," McCoy said, from close to Kirk's shoulder. "We're not here."

Kirk looked, blinked, shook his head. "*You're* not here, Bones," he said. "That's for sure."

"What's that supposed to mean?"

"I can hear you, but I can't see you." In fact, he couldn't see anybody, although he could hear other voices around him. The landscape appeared to be deserted.

"What in the hell are you talking about, Jim? I'm standing right in front of you."

Kirk extended his arm, reaching toward where the doctor's voice seemed to be coming from. He felt nothing.

"Watch the eyes, Jim! I need those."

"Apparently mine aren't good for much. At the moment, anyway." Kirk was trying to project calm. Whatever he and the others were experiencing was almost certainly not real. That lack of reality could have profound consequences, he feared, especially if people became too emotionally invested in their immediate perceptions of reality. He needed to keep the mood light, if he could. "Anybody else needing an eye test?"

"I could use one, Captain," a woman's voice called out. "Unless you really have grown three feet taller in the last five minutes."

"Not that I'm aware of. But anything is possible. Literally, anything."

"Jim—" McCoy said. He was interrupted by another jolt, like a one-note earthquake. Kirk was already growing accustomed to those. He flexed his knees and rode it out, curious as to what would come next.

When his vision cleared, he and the crew were inside the most impossible scene yet. They were once again on the alien ship, which he had always believed was the case, but inside one of the wider corridors. He guessed that they remained in basically the same positions they had been "outside," with two crucial differences.

Some of them were standing on the deck, some on each wall, and some on the overhead—except that each of those *was* the deck; there were no visible walls or ceilings. Everyone noticed at about the same time, and although the effect was disconcerting, the gravity in each position appeared equally strong. Nobody was falling.

The other difference was that this time, they were not alone.

Those mixed in with them were unmistakably Ixtoldans. Kirk recognized their thick-limbed but graceful bodies, the gold-dusted skin, the tight but flowing manner of dress. There must have been thirty of them, in small knots of three or four, standing on all the same unlikely floors as the *Enterprise* crew. They held unheard conversations, walked briskly here or there, and when their paths took them in proximity with the Starfleet personnel, they didn't adjust course or hesitate, but simply walked right through.

"They're not here," Kirk said.

"Not at present," Spock agreed. He was almost directly above Kirk. Or below. "Or what passes for our present."

"This could . . . make a person question his senses."

"If he didn't," McCoy said, "I'd have to question his sanity."

"They are real, though?" Kirk said. "The Ixtoldans?"

"I have no reason to believe otherwise," Spock said.

"Except that they can walk through us."

Spock took four steps to his left and passed through

a pair of Ixtoldan females who appeared to be sharing a private joke. "And we through them."

"We've got to find the others and get off this ship," Kirk said. "We can't do this indefinitely."

"Agreed," McCoy said. "But how do you propose we search for them, when we don't even know where *we* are?"

"I'm . . . still working on that, Bones. As soon as I know, I'll tell you."

"This can't be," Miranda Tikolo said. "It looks just like the Academy."

"It *is* the Academy," Chandler said. "It's the floor I lived on."

"Are you sure?" Greene said. "I mean, it looks familiar, but—"

Chandler ran her fingers across a bluish streak on the wall, about waist high. "I made this mark," she said. "Roughhousing with friends. Mags had just dyed her hair, and it was still damp."

"You know how impossible that is," Ruiz said. "Right?"

Chandler didn't seem to register his comment. She was staring at the third door down from the mark on the wall. She had gone rigid, every muscle as tight as a drum. "Eve," Tikolo said. "Are you . . . ?"

Chandler's gaze was distant, focused not on the door but on something beyond it. Her voice was thin. "That was our room," she said. "Mags . . . she was one of those girls who take things so seriously. Pushed herself, you know? She always had to be the best. She said her parents expected it of her, but I think she expected more from herself than anyone else did."

"Nobody joins the Academy to be second-rate," Greene said.

"It was more than that, for her. She had to be first, best, and brightest. At everything."

"That's a lot of pressure," Tikolo said. She had known people like that at the Academy, too, and after. In some ways, Chandler could have been describing *her*. "Driven" hadn't begun to describe her in those days.

"I was sure Mags could live up to her own standards," Chandler said. "If anybody could. I didn't worry about her. Sometimes I teased her about it. I thought that if I didn't take it too seriously, maybe she would relax a little. Only . . ."

She let the sentence trail off and took a couple of steps closer to the door. Suddenly, Tikolo was afraid Chandler would open it, and she didn't want to see what was on the other side. She didn't know what would be there, but it wouldn't be good. That much, she knew for certain.

"Only what, Eve?" she asked. She moved toward Chandler, to block her from the door if she had to.

"Only she didn't. Instead of relaxing, she got worse. Tense. Afraid. And then . . . then she failed a big exam. I don't even remember what class it was for."

She started to reach for the door, and Tikolo grabbed her arm. "No, Eve," she said. Her certainty grew more powerful. That door had to stay closed, no matter what. "You don't want to go through there."

"I came back to the room after class," Chandler said, as if Tikolo weren't even there. "And I went inside. The lights were out. I called her name. The lights came on and I still didn't see her, but she—" Chandler swallowed back a sob. Tears glistened in her eyes, and one glided down her left cheek. "She was on her bed, up against the wall. The wall was smoking, and so was her head. Her phaser pistol was on the floor."

Tikolo positioned herself between Chandler and the door. Now she knew basically what waited on the other side: Mags, or a reasonable replica thereof. Complete with head halfway blown off by her own phaser. "That was a long time ago, Eve," she said. "There's nothing we need to see in there now. I'm sorry for what happened to Mags, but—"

"Tikolo," Ruiz said. "Any idea who *they* are?"

She looked past Chandler. Ruiz was pointing back down the hall, in the direction they had come from. The hallway seemed much longer now, and shrouded in shadow.

Inside the shadows were figures, hunched over, only their eyes and teeth catching any light at all. They were watching the group, and those teeth looked long and sharp.

Were they real? Was any of this real? If she let Chandler open the door, would Mags be on the other side, or would it be a circus clown, or the surface of the sun?

Tikolo had been afraid before. She knew what it felt like and was alarmed to recognize its return: the hollowness at her core, her guts twisted into knots, her mouth as dry as the floor of a desert, her heart slamming against her chest like an animal that wanted out. She heard the roar of blood in her ears and all she could think was that she had to get away, she had to get out of here before . . .

Before what?

Tikolo didn't know that.

She only knew that all of it, this ship, the Starfleet Academy hallway, the creatures in the darkness, it was all too much.

She knew fear. She was distressingly well acquainted with panic. And panic was returning, rushing up from within her, rising like a tide. When it filled her, if it did, she wouldn't think clearly. Her world would narrow to a single point and nothing would matter except escape.

The captain had put her in charge of this mission. She had to find Bunker and get him back to the rest of the landing party. That meant she had to put aside her worries, quell the panic, and get to work.

She grabbed Chandler again, harder this time. "Come on, Eve. Your Academy days have been over for a long time, and there's nothing behind that door you need to see." Then she pointed her phaser toward the shadowed beings. "And you, I don't know if you're real or not. But I recommend that you don't try to block our way, because we're here from the *Starship Enterprise,* and we're coming through!"

Seventeen

The ship gave another jolt, and James Kirk saw Paul O'Meara standing before him in chain mail and a helmet, a pike in his metal-gloved hands. Behind him a castle rose from a misty plain, its walls made from heavy gray stones. Mounted knights rode across a lowered drawbridge; Kirk thought he recognized Bones at the front of the pack, Romer behind him, then Spock and the rest of the landing party.

A jolt and he was alone, floating in the void of deep space, only it was a negative version. The emptiness was pure dazzling white, the visible stars and planets black spots burning through the white.

A jolt and he was on a windswept landscape that could only be the surface of Vulcan: sheer cliffs in the middle distance with what might have been the constructs of Vulcan hands atop them, vast unbroken plains of ruddy stone, an orange-red sky above.

A jolt and he was back on the bridge of the *Enterprise*. But it was different, bigger, with dozens more display screens lining the walls. He didn't recognize most of the bridge crew, or the uniforms they wore—belted red coats with white detailing, black pants and boots. Those he did know, Chekov and Spock and Uhura and Sulu, were older than the versions he served with.

A jolt and he was on a Starfleet training shuttle, flown by someone he hadn't seen since his Starfleet Academy days and whose name he couldn't bring to mind.

A jolt and he was at the center of a massive city, with buildings blocking out the sky and so many lights blazing against the dark that it seemed night would never fall again.

A jolt and he was in a tunnel, deep underground. Wooden beams held the earth at bay, and glowing rocks, placed at regular intervals, provided illumination. Four-armed creatures that might have been molded from the very clay they worked dug at the ground with rough-hewn wooden shovels.

A jolt and he was once again on the alien ship. The members of the landing party were there, too. Most looked as if they'd been through a war. Haunted eyes, drawn faces, pale skin. In a way, he supposed they had. Not a literal war, but a war against every sense they possessed. He felt the battle fatigue, too, a weariness that seemed to begin at his core and emanate outward.

"We seem . . . stable," he said. "For the moment. Everyone all right?"

"A long way from all right, Captain," McCoy said. "I expect everyone else feels the same way."

Romer shook her head. Her dark hair hung in limp, sweat-soaked curls. "That was the strangest, scariest thing I've ever experienced," she said. "Those—whatever they were—those monsters, with their yellow eyes—"

"No," countered Beachwood. "Their eyes were bright green, like light passing through emeralds."

Kirk hadn't seen either of those things. "Never mind that," he said. "I think we all went different places, saw different sights. Trying to compare will only be more disorienting."

"I can't help worrying about Miranda and the others," O'Meara said. "If they went through that, too, wherever they are."

"We need to track them down," Kirk agreed. He noticed another member of the security force, Jensen, a burly guy with thick, black hair on his head and showing at his collar and cuffs, who was sitting on the deck, his back against a wall, head down between his knees. He was breathing in short, anxious pants, and his hands were trembling uncontrollably. Kirk inclined his head in the man's direction. "Bones."

McCoy met his gaze briefly, nodded once, and went to the man's side, crouching beside him. He placed a hand on the man's arm. "We're all okay, Jensen," he said. "So are you. Whatever happened to you there wasn't—well, I can't say it wasn't real. But it was only momentary. You're here with the rest of us now."

Jensen tried to reply, but he couldn't force words out around his ragged panting.

McCoy reached into the bag he carried on a strap that cut across his chest. "I'm going to give you something that'll calm you down," he said. "Try to take a deep breath, hold it in for a count of three, then release it slowly."

Jensen tried to comply, and as he made the effort, McCoy shot a mild sedative into his arm. The man's breathing started to normalize. "It's just a mild one," McCoy assured the man. "Can't afford to have you going to sleep. You never know when we'll need that strong back."

Jensen showed a smile that was at least half grimace. "Thanks, Doc. I'm good now. I think, anyway."

McCoy helped him to his feet. The others appeared to have largely recovered; most of the blank stares and gaping mouths were gone, replaced by what Kirk considered a determination to get the job done and get home. But a couple were still glassy-eyed, and he caught more than one fighting to contain tremors.

McCoy pulled him aside. "We've got to get this wrapped up, Jim," he said. "Much more of this craziness and we're going to be dealing with some severe psychological trauma."

"We can't just walk out on Bunker and the others, Bones."

"I'm not suggesting that. I'm only saying we need to be quick about it."

Kirk summoned Spock to join the whispered discussion. "What do you think?" he asked. "Can we resume the search party without that happening again?"

"I do not know, Captain," Spock said. As he spoke, Kirk realized that he was as shell-shocked as the rest. His flesh was as pale as Kirk had ever seen it. "I really have no idea how to interpret what just happened. It was most illogical."

"Logic and this damn ship have nothing to do with each other," McCoy said.

"Maybe not," Kirk said. "But we're here and we have to address the situation as it stands. I was hoping maybe you had recognized a pattern that eluded me, Mister Spock."

"No pattern at all," Spock said.

"You hate that, don't you?" McCoy asked.

"I would not use the word 'hate' to describe—"

"That's *exactly* the word. You love logic, and we've gone down the rabbit hole and left logic behind. You look for patterns, because they're a way of making sense of the universe, and where we are there is no sense."

Spock seemed to realize that McCoy wasn't taunting him, but trying to engage him. His eyes focused on the doctor's worn, comfortable face. "You are correct, Doctor," he said. "I suppose I do hate this ship, if that is how you define the word. I wish we had never come."

"I think that goes for all of us," Kirk said. He took out his communicator, ready to try again even though he knew what the outcome would be. "Let's get off it as soon as we can, shall we?"

"Look out!" Greene shouted. He shoved Ruiz into the nearest bulkhead.

"What the hell, man?" Ruiz responded. He had a bright red spot on his cheek, where it had been slammed against the wall.

"That thing was about to hit you," Greene said. "You didn't see it?"

"I didn't see a thing except you ramming into me. What thing?"

"Like a bat," Greene said. "Only not really. It was bigger, like a big bird, but it had those kind of leathery wings and erratic flight, like a bat."

"There was no bat," Vandella said. "I was looking right at you guys. If there had been a big bat, I'd have seen it."

"Not me," Chandler said. "Those other guys were blocking my view."

"What guys?" Vandella asked.

"Those ones from the shadows."

Tikolo didn't like the direction the conversation was heading. The beings in the shadows had vanished the first time she'd fired her phaser at them. But since then, they'd been visited by all sorts of apparitions, and she was no longer certain what was real and what wasn't.

They had left the corridor that seemed to be a Starfleet Academy hallway, but somehow they found themselves deep in the bowels of the ship, surrounded by equipment she couldn't even understand: tall racks of computers that went on for what seemed like kilometers, pipes that snaked in every direction, huge banks of gears caked with sludge. Now they were passing through a narrow tube, barely wide enough for them to walk two abreast. All hope of finding Bunker had fled; their only remaining goal was to locate anything familiar so they could get back to the rest of the crew.

As they made their way through the mechanical maze, semitransparent creatures had emerged from the walls, then disappeared again. They had heard the great, anguished sobs of a weeping woman, but when they rounded the corner behind which she should be waiting, the sound had stopped and there was no one in sight. And now, apparently, different people were seeing different things, instead of all of them experiencing the same vision.

Nearing the end of the tube—beyond, Tikolo could see that it opened into a cavernous, dimly lit space, though she could see no detail beyond that— she heard the unmistakable sound of a door opening and slamming shut. An old-fashioned door, like the one her grandparents had had in their home when she was a girl, made of wood with hinges of brass that squeaked unless her grandfather remembered to lubricate them.

"That can't be," she said.

"What?" Vandella was right behind her.

"That sound. It's a door. Hear it?"

"Yes, but I couldn't place it."

The door creaked on its hinges as it opened. Then it squealed, shorter but louder, and banged shut.

"There could not possibly be a door like that on this ship," Vandella said. "Could there?"

"The ship looks pretty old," Tikolo said. "Doesn't seem likely, but who knows?" She started walking faster, hoping to spot the door when she cleared the tunnel.

Because the last thing she needed was for there to be no door. It helped that Vandella had heard it, too. Helped a little.

She had been fighting against the terror that threatened to engulf her, but every apparition, every audio hallucination, everything that looked or sounded or felt real but wasn't, made her fight that much harder.

If she discovered that there was no door—or perhaps just as bad, that there was a door but it was opening and closing on its own—that might just be the thing that would finally break her.

"Miranda," Vandella said as she approached the tunnel's end. "Are you holding it together?"

"What does it look like, Stanley?"

"You look tense. Like your muscles are stretched too tight. You need to relax a little."

She whirled on him, heedless of the others coming up behind. "*Relax*? Do you even understand how absurd that is?"

"I don't mean you should kick off your boots and take a nap. But you're too wound up. You're not at your best, and you need to be."

"So that'll help. Criticizing me. That's perfect."

"That's not my intent, Miranda, you know that."

"I used to think I knew a lot of things. I'm not so sure anymore. Not so sure about anything."

He moved in close, held her arms, and lowered his voice so only she could hear. "You can be sure that I love you, Miranda. I just want you to be safe."

She wrenched her arms from his grasp and caught herself before she drove a fist into his throat. "Damn it, you did *not* just say that! Now? Come on, Stanley, think!"

"What? I—"

Tikolo punched his arm, pulling the blow so she didn't give it the full force she wanted to, then turned away from him and hurried the rest of the way through the tunnel. At the end, she emerged into a large space, mostly empty, but with a few pyramid-shaped structures in the middle and lots of open air above them. She heard the door bang shut one more time, and then it went silent.

But there was no door. There was no door and she was lost and she didn't know what to do anymore.

And the panic? The panic was going to win.

That outcome was no longer in question.

Eighteen

"I canna understand why she's so dead-set on destroyin' that big ship," Scotty said. "She's just been after me about it again."

He had met with Chan'ya and Gonzales in his quarters, where he had gone for a quick nap. He'd been asleep for less than ten minutes when they came calling, and after they'd left he had not been able to fall asleep again. A man needed his sleep, he knew that. He needed to keep his wits about him, to stay alert and sharp. The landing party had been gone for hours.

"It's beyond me," Sulu said. He somehow managed to look just as crisp as ever, as if he had slept for eight hours, showered, and eaten a full meal. Scotty knew that wasn't the case. With the captain gone, Scotty had been spending more time than usual on the bridge and less in engineering, and every time he stepped onto the bridge, Sulu was there, in his place at the helm. "But I am no expert on Ixtoldan customs or psychology."

"I'm not sure there is such a thing as Ixtoldan psychology," Chekov offered. "They all seem crazy as loons to me."

"We probably seem the same to them, Pavel," Uhura said. She had spun around in her seat so she faced into the bridge. "We can't judge what we don't understand."

Scotty lowered himself wearily into the captain's chair. "I knew Captain Kirk had a hard job," he said. "But I never appreciated how hard, before. It's all I can do not to throw the lot of 'em into the brig and let 'em rot."

"I do find it disturbing," Sulu said, "that the Federation seems so eager to admit them, yet they seem so ready to embrace a violent solution. They are certainly not the peace-loving people we were told about when the mission began."

"They believe the ship is abandoned, though," Uhura reminded them. "They're not saying we should destroy an inhabited vessel."

"I suppose not," Scotty said. "Still—"

"So we should be trying to figure out what that ship represents to them that makes them so anxious to vaporize it. If it's not some*body* they want to destroy, then it must be some*thing*," Uhura offered.

"But then you're back to trying to figure out the Ixtoldans," Chekov said. "And that just can't be done."

"Has anyone tried asking them?"

Sulu smiled. "Uhura, you just might have something there."

"That's all well and good," Scotty said. He closed

his eyes and leaned back in the chair. "But who'll do the askin'?" Nobody answered, and after a few seconds, he opened his eyes again. "What are you all lookin' at me for?"

"Captain?" O'Meara said. They had made it down two decks, but they were taking it slow, stopping and listening for signs of life, checking as many doors as they could. It was a big ship, and searching this way took time. But they couldn't take a chance on missing anyone; because the ship was so huge, backtracking would take longer than moving cautiously in the first place.

"Yes, Mister O'Meara?"

"I don't think we're alone here."

"Explain."

"It's just a feeling, sir. You know, when you feel like there's someone watching you? Or just somebody in the room? You can't see them or hear them, but you know there's someone there."

"I'm familiar with it."

"Well, I've had it since we got here. Instead of going away, it's been getting stronger."

"Me too, sir," Romer said.

"Anybody else?"

Hands went up. Most of the group, including McCoy. Spock didn't raise his hand, but his right eyebrow arched slightly and he gave a subtle but unmistakable nod.

"I've felt it, too," Kirk admitted. "Given everything else that's been going on, I wasn't sure if I could trust my own instincts. But if we're unanimous, then it's probably safe to say that something's on this ship with us."

"What do you think it is, Captain?" Jensen asked.

"I don't think any of us can know that," Kirk said. He led the way through an open door, into a shadowed chamber that looked as if it had been a mess hall. Tables and benches that humans—or Ixtoldans—could have used were jumbled against the far wall as if they'd slid there and piled up in random fashion. He felt, in a visceral way, someone standing directly in front of him, as if daring him to pass. He could almost feel hot breath on his face. But there was no physical presence, and he pushed past whatever it was.

O'Meara was right, though.

They weren't alone.

Romer came in behind Kirk, then McCoy, then Gao. Kirk was looking around the room, thinking that maybe if he didn't try so hard to focus on what couldn't be seen, he might be able to catch something out of the corner of his eye. He watched the crew members pass through the doorway. Gao had barely made it inside when some unseen force knocked him off his feet.

"Gao!" Kirk shouted. He moved toward the man, but something blocked his way. As he tried to bull past it he saw Gao lifted bodily from the floor—by what, he still couldn't tell—and hurled back down again. Gao cried out in obvious agony, struggling against his invisible foe. His face was going from red to purple, and Kirk could tell he was being choked.

Kirk body-slammed his invisible blocker, and felt something unseen give beneath his charge. He continued on toward Gao, but strong hands gripped his arms and shoulders, even twining in his hair, and yanked him back. Other members of the team were similarly hindered. They cried out, fought with everything they could. Kirk fired his phaser at a target he couldn't see but whose heft he experienced in every muscle that he strained trying to break away from it. The beam from his weapon passed through whatever was there and struck an empty stretch of wall behind it. For the briefest of instants, he thought the grip loosened. He wrenched his right arm free and aimed the phaser again, this time toward where he believed—from the position of Gao's strained form—his attacker was.

But it was no good. There were others directly behind. If the phaser beam missed, he would hit his own people. And given that they were under assault by seemingly shapeless, noncorporeal beings that still, somehow, had the ability to physically interact with them, he didn't dare so much as stun a member of his crew. He would need every hand available.

And, he saw now, it was too late to help Gao. The

man had gone limp, any motion simply the result of the force that still squeezed his neck. His eyes bulged from their sockets, his mouth gaped, and his throat was distorted by the presence of unseen hands.

Kirk raged against his impossible tethers. "Let me go!" he shouted. He yanked his left shoulder loose, almost tearing the gold fabric of his shirt, then spun and delivered a roundhouse right with all his weight behind it. To his satisfaction, he felt an impact, faint but there nonetheless, and he was free.

He rushed toward Gao again. As he got close, he converted his momentum into a flying kick, aimed just above the crewman. And again he connected with something less than solid but more than nothing. Gao fell to the deck.

Then everybody was released, and they gathered around Gao. McCoy shoved the others aside and examined the man. After several long seconds, he looked up at Kirk and shook his head slowly. "He's dead, Jim."

"But . . . how? What were those things?"

"Ghosts," O'Meara speculated.

"Aliens," Beachwood said. "Noncorporeal but sentient."

"The latter is more likely," Spock agreed. "However, without more data, a definitive answer cannot be known."

Kirk scanned the big room. He had not seen their

attackers before, and nothing had changed in that regard. "I feel like they're gone."

"So do I," Jensen said. "Before, the hairs on the back of my neck were standing up."

Given the volume of that hair, Kirk thought, *that would be an alarm hard to ignore.*

"Bunker's not here," he said. "Neither is the search party." Another problem had just presented itself: now they had a corpse. He would not leave Gao's body behind, but neither did he want anyone to have to carry it while they continued searching the ship. They could leave an electronic beacon behind, but they couldn't trust it to function correctly. "Everybody make a mental note of this location," he announced. "We'll return for Mister Gao on the way back to the shuttles."

They continued moving through the ship, looking for the rest of their team, Kirk trying his communicator every few minutes. As they searched, he summoned Spock and McCoy closer. "We've encountered noncorporeal beings before," he said. "But they don't make sense here."

"What do you mean?" McCoy asked.

"Why would they have tables and chairs? Doors that open and close by hand? Controls that use dials and buttons and switches?"

"Good point."

"And," Spock pointed out, "they have made no serious attempt to communicate with us. A single attack hardly counts as communication."

"That we know of," Kirk corrected. "If they're so alien that we simply can't understand them, we might not recognize attempts to open a dialogue. But yes, I think you're right—whatever is aboard this ship with us is decidedly malevolent."

"Mister O'Meara might have had a point," Spock said.

"*You* think they're ghosts?" McCoy asked.

"I think we cannot dismiss the idea out of hand."

"Now I really have heard everything. Our logical first officer believes in ghosts."

"I believe there is much about the dimensional fold that we do not yet understand. What we do know about it suggests that the laws of physics that we take for granted do not apply here. Further, there has long been speculation that ghosts are simply electrical impulses that flee the body at death. Nothing that is can become nothing at all. Even electricity has to go somewhere."

"I'll grant you that," Kirk said. He pushed open a door, stuck his head into a storage closet of some kind, filled with gear he couldn't recognize. "So would these ghosts be the remnants of the original occupants of the ship?"

"That is one possibility. Keep in mind, there are other ships joined with this one. Including the *McRaven*."

Kirk's thoughts had been moving in that direction, but Spock had gotten there first. The idea of ghosts was hard to accept, but as the Vulcan had pointed out, the ordinary rules weren't followed here. But the ghosts of his fellow Starfleet personnel, so recently alive and rushing through space on a ship virtually identical to the *Enterprise*? That was an even more disturbing concept. "Why would they attack us?"

"I've got an idea on that score," McCoy said. "As you know, I've been brushin' up on psychology recently."

In part, to effectively monitor and treat Miranda Tikolo, Kirk knew. She was a good addition to the crew, but she was dealing with a unique set of problems. "Go ahead, Bones."

"Well, some of what I've been reading talks about different theories of the mind. One twentieth-century Earth theory held that consciousness is present when a critical mass of electrical impulses reaches a certain level of activity and organization. By that standard—since we know by instrumentation and observation that there are such impulses on this ship—we can theorize that perhaps they have reached that level. They're contained within the ship, which could count as organization."

"So you're speculating that the ship itself is conscious?" Kirk asked.

"I'm just sayin', it's not an idea we should dismiss out of hand."

"Mister Spock?" Spock had paused outside another door. "Thoughts?"

"The doctor's analysis appears sound."

"And there's one more thing," McCoy said.

"What's that?"

"If this ship is conscious?"

"Yes?"

"It's as mad as a box of frogs."

Nineteen

"Coming, Mister Spock?"

The captain stood just off his left shoulder. The away team had passed him by as he stood beside a doorway. The logical thing to do was to open the door and see what was inside, but as yet he had not been able to do so.

"Yes, Captain. But—"

"Yes?"

Spock didn't answer. He couldn't define exactly what he was experiencing—another insubstantial presence, he believed, but not an aggressive one, this time. Instead, he felt immersed in a warm, welcoming psychic bath. It—he had a vague sense of *she*—wanted him to accompany it. He was suspicious, but the overwhelming sensation was calming, confidently reassuring. "Captain, I believe . . . I believe that this being wants me to go with it. With her. Into this room."

"Are you sure, Spock? We can just check it and move on."

"There is something different here," Spock replied. "This presence is not like those we have previously encountered. And there is a sense of urgency I cannot resist."

"I'll leave someone here with you," Kirk said. "We have to come back this way anyway, to retrieve Mister Gao."

"That is not necessary."

"We at least have to look inside."

Spock opened the door and peered into a room containing shelves of physical books, and computer stations surrounded by what looked like some sort of storage media arranged on racks.

"It's a library," McCoy said.

"So it would appear. Perhaps here, I can learn more about our situation."

"You can't read Ixtoldan, Spock."

"You are only partially correct, Doctor. I cannot read Ixtoldan *yet*."

"I don't like it, Spock," Kirk said. "Dividing up our forces more seems like a bad idea."

"I understand your concern, and its validity. Nonetheless, this presence assures me that this is where I need to be."

"When we come back, we don't even know if this room will be here," McCoy argued. "It could be a cornfield or a nightclub or something."

"The hope of learning something valuable has to take precedence over less likely possibilities. I am convinced that I will be safe here."

The captain's jaw worked. He wanted to say

something more, but he seemed to recognize that Spock's mind would not be changed. "All right," he said at last. "But don't go anywhere."

Spock didn't answer. The presence was tugging him, almost bodily, into the library. Behind him, Kirk and McCoy went to rejoin the rest of the group, waiting to advance down the corridor. Spock passed through the doorway and was flooded by a surprising, almost thoroughly human emotion.

He felt as if he had come home.

Miranda Tikolo was hopelessly lost.

Trying to retrace their steps, the team had instead found themselves in an area of narrow passageways between rusted steel walls inset with gauges and dials and even hand cranks that all served a purpose she could not begin to discern. The ceilings were so low that Chandler could reach up and brush them with her fingertips. The course twisted and hooked back on itself and felt, to Tikolo's hyperactively anxious mind, like an ambush waiting to happen.

With every step, she fought to quell her rising panic. It would be easy to give up, to accept that they would never again find Captain Kirk and the rest. The ship was impossible, its physical properties constantly in flux. Her heart was thudding rapidly in her chest and ears and throat, her breathing was shallow, and she had a hard time holding on to a thought for more than an instant.

But the captain had put her in charge, and until she could no longer function, she had to do her duty.

"This section can't last forever," she said, although it felt like it already had. "I guess we're in engineering or something, but we'll get back to the crew decks soon enough."

"What about Bunker?" Greene asked.

"He's on his own, I'm afraid. For all we know, he's already found the others."

"I guess that's possible."

"Of course it is." Tikolo turned yet another corner and looked down an incredibly long, straight stretch, still narrow but with dark spaces along its length that might have been side passages. Terror welled up again; anything might be lurking in those shadows.

Then the ship gave a powerful lurch and everything turned black. The floor fell away beneath her feet and a rasping scream tore from her throat.

Light returned in brilliant flashes, showing a range of scenes that could not be: the nearby surface of a sun, with flares reaching out toward her; a tunnel formed of pure color, shifting and blending faster than thought; a thick, lush jungle draped in mosses and vines, birds screeching in alarm.

The darkness came back abruptly, and this time it stayed. Tikolo wasn't falling, but neither could she detect any solid surface beneath her feet. She was suspended in the complete absence of everything.

And it wasn't the first time.

The shuttle, off Outpost 4. Same thing. She had killed all her power so the Romulans wouldn't detect her. The tiny craft had been floating in space, the blackness inside it absolute. After several hours, the oxygen had grown thin and she had restored enough power to stay alive, but not enough to turn on any lights or gravity or other comforts.

All the while, the Romulans had been pounding the outposts, obliterating them, one after the next. Killing everyone she knew there, everyone she had worked with.

While she waited, floating, in the dark.

Abruptly, the lights came back on.

And there they were.

"Romulans!" she screamed.

"Where?" Greene asked.

"Miranda!" Chandler cried. "There aren't any Romulans here!"

"Didn't you feel that impact? Their phaser batteries are pummeling us!"

"Those bumps have been happening since we got here," Vandella said. "They're atmospheric disturbances or something, not Romulan phasers." He put a hand on her shoulder that she supposed was meant to be soothing.

She brushed it off. "You don't know that! How could you?"

"Miranda, I know because I've been here as long as you have. They come and they go, and when they come strange things happen. Like this." He waved a hand at their surroundings: a stark white laboratory space. The equipment that had once been used here was scattered around the place, smashed into pieces so small they weren't recognizable. The room itself had been spared the decay and seemingly organic growth that had taken over most of the ship.

"What about it?"

"Don't you remember? Before, we were in a long, tight hallway of some kind. Then it went dark, and now here we are. Completely different place. Romulans didn't do that. It's the dimensional fold, that's all."

"Aaagk!" She let out a brutal, wordless cry and whipped her head from side to side. "Liar! Stop it!"

"We're on your side, Miranda," Chandler assured her. "We're just trying to get back to the captain, that's all."

Tikolo thought she knew the people who were talking to her, but their names fled from her consciousness and she was suddenly not so sure. Their faces no longer looked familiar, and then they no longer looked human at all. They were shape-shifters, pretending to be her comrades, to get her guard down. They were, no doubt, in league with the Romulans outside, punishing the starship from the safety of their bird-of-prey.

She broke free from the circle they'd made around her, ignoring their shouts and their phony concerned expressions, and darted for the nearest door.

"Miranda!" somebody cried. She didn't stop. The doorway was just ahead; she raised her arms and battered through it. On the other side, she burst into a wide lobby-type area, with staircases joining the decks above and below.

Behind her, she heard the clatter of running feet, and those people, her so-called friends, flooded into the lobby.

And from the staircase leading up, Romulan soldiers opened fire.

Twenty

Kirk and his team left Spock, reluctantly, and continued their search. They had cleared the deck they were on, so they had started down the ladder to the one below when they heard the sound of shuffling feet, the soft creaks and rustles of uniforms, even a murmur of quiet voices.

"Tikolo?" Kirk called. "Bunker? Who's there?"

The response was a guttural shout, and the careful footfalls changed to the sound of running feet.

"That's not Tikolo," Kirk said.

"That was Romulan, sir," Romer said.

"We're a long way from the Romulan Neutral Zone. Are you sure?"

"Aye, sir."

"Retreat," Kirk said. He was less than halfway down the ladder, and most of the away team had not started down it yet. Better to stick to the high ground than to split their forces. "Retreat!"

Romer, and Beachwood above her, scrambled back up. Kirk followed close behind, drawing his phaser as he reached the deck. "I don't know how many there are," he reported. "But there appear to be Romulans heading this way."

The Romulans might have been just another illusion, but they couldn't afford to count on that. They took cover behind ruined fixtures and other debris, weapons pointed toward the top of the ladder. A few moments later, a dark-haired head appeared there, with arching brows over dark eyes. Three phaser beams blasted it, and the Romulan fell heavily to the deck below.

Almost immediately, the sounds of Romulan disruptors welled up from below, and the deck shook with the force of the weapons' beams hitting it. Those certainly seemed real. Given the condition of the ship, Kirk knew, it was only a matter of time before those guns tore through the flooring and exposed them.

"Return fire!" Kirk called.

A couple of his people moved closer to the opening, so they could fire through it. Disrupter blasts came back up; Jensen had to dive to the side to avoid one. More of them pounded against the floor.

Kirk went as close to the opening as he dared. "How many, Jensen?" he asked.

"I saw four."

Kirk held his phaser at arm's length and poked it into the opening, firing several times in a loose figure-eight pattern. He heard someone cry out in pain. As he was shooting, he risked a hurried glimpse over the side.

He saw five Romulans, wearing battle armor. Two were already down. One pointed up at him and growled a warning, but Kirk drew his head back before he fired.

Three remaining. Of course, he didn't know how many there might be beyond his angle of view.

But they were down there, and he and his crew were up here. They couldn't come up, but he couldn't go down.

Disruptor blasts continued to hammer the floor. If they broke through, he realized, then the Starfleet personnel could fire phasers down through the holes, with more accuracy than those shooting up from below.

"Help them out," he said. He aimed his phaser down at one of the spots he believed the Romulans were targeting, and demonstrated. Sparks flew as the phaser's beam chewed through the flooring material.

In another moment, he'd made a hole. Others in his crew did the same. A disruptor blast came up through the hole, but harmlessly continued toward the ceiling above. As soon as it was gone, Kirk jammed his phaser into the opening and fired at the Romulan aiming his way. The soldier fell. Kirk rushed away before the returning fire came, but then phaser beams from other weapons, also angling down through holes in the floor, took out the last two Romulans.

Kirk peered through the hole again, shifting his view to encompass as much of the lower deck as possible. "That looks like all of them," he said.

"It could be a trap," McCoy warned.

"Could be. But we have to find out. Petty Officer Tikolo and the others are down there somewhere."

"Unless the Romulans got them, too," Beachwood said.

"Don't!" O'Meara blurted out.

"I'm just saying—"

"They're fine," O'Meara said. "I know they're fine."

"We'll never find out if we don't go down," Beachwood observed.

"I'll go first," O'Meara said. "Cover me."

He started for the ladder. Kirk stepped into his way. "I'll go first, Mister O'Meara. You cover me."

O'Meara looked as though he wanted to argue, but he reined it in. "Aye, sir."

Kirk returned to the ladder and started down once again. This time, he kept his phaser in his hand, and as soon as his head cleared the deck, he bent over, almost double, to look for any more living Romulans. He didn't see any, and the dead ones looked very dead, indeed. He descended another step, and then another, his back to the ladder, looking in every direction with every rung he reached.

There did not appear to be any more Romulans. Which raised a series of significant questions. Where had the Romulans come from? Outside the fold? And how? If they had come past the *Enterprise*—*well, scratch that*, he thought, *Scotty wouldn't have let them come past him*.

But the very existence of the fold opened up new

possibilities. The question might have been less *Where* did they come from? and more *When* did they come from? The past? The future? The uniforms and weaponry he could see as he stepped off the final rung looked contemporary, but they could have come as easily from yesterday or tomorrow as next year or a hundred years ago.

That question was not likely to be answered soon. Nor were the others: What were they doing here? Had they been able to navigate within the fold, or had they been attracted by the Ixtoldan ship's apparent gravitational field? Did they know there were Starfleet personnel aboard, or had Kirk's shout been their first indication that they weren't alone? Had they been here when the Starfleet shuttles landed, their cloaking devices somehow concealing their presence? There had been what looked like a Romulan bird-of-prey, attached to the cluster of ships gathered around the Ixtoldan one. But they couldn't have cloaked this ship, even if they had been able to prevent Starfleet instruments from reading their own. So they hadn't been on board the Ixtoldan vessel when it had been scanned.

The most important questions, though, were: Were there really only five? And had the other team, or the missing Mister Bunker, encountered any?

"All clear," he said. "Come on down."

The others descended one at a time. Jensen came last, and he paused at the top of the ladder. "What about Mister Spock, Captain? Should we make sure he's safe?"

Kirk considered the question briefly. Spock was not only the best science officer he had ever known or heard about, he was also a friend, and a very close one. He would no more want something to happen to the Vulcan than he would want to lose his own life.

But sending someone back to stand guard over him would mean further dividing their small group. Any Romulan attack that could defeat Spock could almost as easily defeat Spock and one other, and he only had seven people left, including himself, which meant he could spare no more than two at the outside. And they still had to find Tikolo and her group, and Bunker.

Besides, they had searched that deck, and the one above it, thoroughly, finding no Romulans. The only Romulans so far encountered had come up from below. If any more tried to get up to where Spock was, they would have to go through Kirk and the others.

Finally, there had been the look on Spock's face when he sent them away. He had looked comfortable, at perfect ease. Something—some aspect of this mad, mad starship, Kirk guessed—had convinced him of his safety.

And one of the things one could safely say about Mister Spock was that he was hard to fool. If his safety had been guaranteed, that guarantee could likely be trusted.

"No, Mister Jensen," Kirk finally said. "Mister Spock is fine. We keep searching."

"Aye, aye, sir," Jensen said. As he descended the ladder and stepped onto the deck, he looked a little relieved. Kirk knew that his question had been more than that: it had been an offer that, if accepted, would have required him to return by himself to the library where they'd left Spock. Kirk didn't blame him for not wanting to make that trip; on this ship, he wouldn't want to, either.

They moved carefully toward the dead Romulans. Kirk nudged one with his toe, to make sure the corpse had substance and wasn't simply one more construct thrown his way by the dimensional fold. It did, or seemed to, though he knew the evidence offered by touch could be no more fully trusted than that of any other sense. He wished there were some other way to confirm their reality, but the tricorders couldn't be trusted. He gathered up their weapons, which seemed solid enough. Romer joined him. "Should we bring these with us, sir?" she asked.

"No, I think our phasers are adequate," he said. "I just don't want anyone else who might pass through here to find them. At least, not without a struggle." He cast his gaze about the visible part of the deck and saw a pile of clutter—broken-up furniture, he guessed—in one corner. "There," he said. "We'll toss them into that mess."

He and Romer carried them over and did as he

said. The disruptors blended with the debris, until even he could barely see them there. "Good enough," he said.

Everything about this deck was smaller than the one above it; the corridors were narrower, the ceilings and doorways lower. Even the lighting seemed less bright, though he couldn't tell if that was because the walls were darker or more covered in that moss or mold he was quickly getting used to, or if the change was real.

"We can be sure they're not in the immediate area," he said, "or they'd have heard the fight."

"Which way, Captain?" Beachwood asked.

All these decisions, Kirk thought. *If I weren't here they'd make them without hesitation. Since I am, they have to ask.* It was a captain's lot, he knew. And he didn't mind, not really.

But some days, it was more tiresome than others.

Twenty-one

Scotty had enjoyed the noisy chaos of engineering—so restful, compared to the relative quiet of the bridge—for less than an hour before Uhura's voice came over the intercom, summoning him back. She kept her voice level, as she always did, but he detected a hint of urgency there just the same. "I'm comin', lassie," he replied. *Ought to have my head examined, is what I ought to do,* he thought. *I wonder if I can get myself demoted? And how soon?*

When he exited the turbolift, he was pleasantly surprised to see no Federation diplomats or Ixtoldans in evidence. Maybe this wouldn't be so bad, after all. One look at the glum faces confronting him, though, disabused him of that hope. If the matter hadn't been sensitive, they wouldn't have called him up. He felt the knot in his stomach, which his time in engineering had only begun to unsnarl, start to form again.

"What?" he asked gruffly. "You all look like ye've lost your favorite sheepdog." A sudden, terrible thought flashed through his mind.

Uhura must have seen it on his face. "Oh, no,"

she said quickly. "It's nothing like that. It's just—the Ixtoldan battle cruiser refuses to respond to my hails."

"Hang 'em, then," Scotty said. "They dinna want to talk, then we got nothin' to say to them."

"I'm afraid we do, Mister Scott," Chekov said.

"Why's that, Mister Chekov?"

"Because, sir, our instruments show that they're routing power to their weapons systems."

"Say that again, Mister Chekov. Nice and slow, if you please."

"The Ixtoldan cruiser is powering up its weapons systems."

"I see." Scotty dropped into the captain's chair and swiveled toward Uhura. "And you'd like to ask them why."

"That's correct, sir," Uhura said.

"And they won't answer."

"Also correct."

Scotty gave the situation another moment's thought. "Put me through," he said. "I dinna care if they respond, just make sure they can hear me."

Uhura's fingers flew across her control pad. She nodded once to Scotty.

"Ahoy the *Ton'bey*," Scotty said. "This is Montgomery Scott, acting captain of the *U.S.S. Enterprise*. I know you can hear me, so listen up. I dinna know what ye think you're doin', but it's my duty as a Starfleet officer to warn ye that any discharge of weapons, anywhere in this vicinity, will be considered by Starfleet to be an act of war."

He left that statement hanging there for a long moment, in case the Ixtoldans chose to respond. When they didn't answer, he went on. "We know you're shunting power to your weapons. There's usually only one reason for that. So again, I'm tellin' you, do *not* discharge those weapons. Power them down immediately, or face the consequences. And next time Lieutenant Uhura hails you, answer her. D'ye hear me?"

No answer, still.

"*Enterprise* out," Scotty said. He slashed his hand across his throat, and Uhura broke the connection.

"They heard me, right?" he asked.

"Their ship received the transmission," Uhura said. "I can't tell you if anybody was listening."

He had never expected to utter the sentence that followed. "Well, get Minister Chan'ya up here, then. Let's see if they'll listen to her."

He turned in the chair, facing the front viewscreen. The fold was dead ahead, shifting colors and turning slowly in space as he watched. Somewhere in there—presumably in the ship he could see at its very center, the monstrosity that had sucked in the others like a giant magnet—was the person who belonged in this seat. And the science officer, the irascible doctor, and others. Those people were precious to Montgomery Scott, and he would be damned if he would let some Ixtoldan with an itchy trigger finger put them in harm's way. He would blow the *Ton'bey* out of space before he would let that happen.

When Chan'ya arrived, she was not alone. She was, as usual, accompanied by her retinue. At least she had not brought any of the Federation diplomats for backup, Scotty was glad to note. But she had brought those two tall, thin Ixtoldans, the ones who looked like they could topple over at any moment.

Chan'ya gathered her skirts and stepped onto the bridge like it was her own private throne room and the officers there a flock of court jesters. The tall ones teetered along behind her. "Someone here requested our presence?" Chan'ya said.

"Aye," Scotty replied. "'Twas me."

"Why?"

He pointed in the general direction of the *Ton'bey*. "Your friends on that cruiser over there are powerin' up their weapons," he said. "They've got to stop."

"If that is true, they doubtless have ample reason."

"They've got no reason at all. D'you see another ship around here that looks like a threat?"

"We have no instruments of our own," Chan'ya said. "We can see only what you want us to see; therefore, we have no way to verify what you say."

"Then you'll just have to trust me, won't ye? Is that so hard for you to do?"

One of the tall Ixtoldans ventured a few steps forward. "Mister Scott, you would be advised to remember whom you are addressing."

"I know perfectly well who I'm addressing, you animated pair of stilts. Now you keep out of this. I'm talkin' to your boss."

"There is no need for angry words, Mister Scott," Chan'ya said.

"The hell there isn't! You talk to the captain of that ship, now, and tell 'im to stand down. If ye won't do it, so help me, I'll load you into the first torpedo tube I fire at him!"

"Mister Scott," Uhura said. She didn't need to say more. The tone of her voice and the warning in her eyes carried the message clearly. Scotty was a human being with all the usual baggage, but he was also an officer of Starfleet. As such, he had a different set of responsibilities. The man in him wanted to use the two taller Ixtoldans for kindling, and maybe get a good fire going under Chan'ya, but the Starfleet officer recognized his duty. "I apologize, ma'am," he said. "I let my emotions get away from me. Our science officer, who's over on that ship right now, would tell you that's a common human failing. I dinna see it that way, but I admit that I should have used better judgment, and I'm sorry."

"Well and good, Mister Scott." She did not sound contrite or forgiving, but then she always sounded the same to him: as if she were talking to something she had to scrape off her shoe.

"So you'll talk to the captain?"

"We do not know why he is, as you say, powering

up the weapons. If indeed he is. We are afraid the captain of the *Ton'bey* is not someone we know well or talk to often. If we tried now, we would doubtless get the same response that you did."

"I got nothin' at all."

"There you are. The very same."

"So he won't take your hails either?"

"We cannot remember the last time we spoke. Probably when a Starfleet shuttle picked us up from Earth orbit to carry us to Federation headquarters."

"Are there others on the ship, then, that you and your party are in better contact with?"

"We are afraid not. We are quite isolated here on your starship. Not uncomfortable, mind you. But isolated from our own kind, yes."

She was lying to him, and he knew it. He was well aware of every communications signal entering or leaving the *Enterprise,* and he knew that she—at least, someone in her party, using her quarters—was in touch with the *Ton'bey* several times a day. Granted, he couldn't tell if those communications were reaching the battle cruiser's commander, but he had no reason to think otherwise.

He wanted to shake her, to demand that she at the very least respect his intelligence. His earlier blowup had softened him, though. He would not do that again, and he would not lay hands on his captain's guests. *His* guests, until the away team returned.

"No communication?" he asked, giving her one more chance to come clean. "You're certain of that?"

She didn't take it. "Quite certain, yes. The difference between none and some is hardly a distinction we would fail to grasp."

"I'm sure not." Not that he had trusted her before, but now he would trust her even less. He was almost certain that she was lying. And if she wasn't, then she had a turncoat in her midst, someone talking to the *Ton'bey* without her knowledge or consent.

Either way, he had to stay wary of them all.

"Will there be anything else, Mister Scott?"

"No, that's it," he said. "Sorry to have bothered you."

"Well and good." She said that a lot, he had noted. It was as if she had to give the world permission to continue doing whatever it wanted to do.

He watched the retinue board the turbolift. The door closed, and they were gone.

"Guess I got carried away, didn't I?"

"A bit," Uhura admitted. "Not that anyone could blame you."

"I was hoping you'd go through with it," Chekov said. "I'd love to push the button when you launch her."

"Believe me, I was givin' it some serious thought." He held up his right hand and eyed the gold braided stripes on his red sleeve. "It'd cost me these, but damned if it might not be worth the sacrifice." He pushed himself from the chair, more comfortable by far than his usual perch in engineering. There were some benefits to command, after all. Catching Uhura's eye, he said, "Tell Mister Gonzales that I'll see him in his quarters in five minutes. And he'll be alone."

"Right away, Mister Scott."

He went to the turbolift. When the door whooshed open, he stopped and turned back toward the bridge crew. "And thank you," he said. "All of you, for your support." He shook his head. "Our captain does nae have an easy job."

When he activated the buzzer on the door of the quarters assigned to Gonzales, anger had begun once again to seep through Scott's thin veneer of control. He wasn't sure if folks were trying to play him because the captain was away, or if they would have been every bit as ornery with Captain Kirk as they were with him. He suspected the former, though, and it made his blood boil.

The door opened and Scotty went in. Gonzales was sitting at a computer station, but he rose and extended a hand in greeting. Scotty shook it.

"Will you sit, Mister Scott?" Gonzales asked. "Options are limited, I'm afraid, but—"

"I'm not stayin' long, Mister Gonzales."

"I see. This is not a social call, then?"

"Between engineering and command duties, I've little time for socializin'."

"Of course."

"Before I say any more, I want to remind you of

who you represent. The United Federation of Planets, not Ixtolde. I understand your mission is to make nice with 'em, but you remember who you are sworn to serve?"

"Of course," Gonzales said again. He returned to his chair by the computer.

"Here's the thing. Minister Chan'ya's lyin' to us. The *Ton'bey* is routing power to its weapons systems. They're no doubt fully powered up and ready to go. That's only done when a fight is in the offin', and far as I can tell, there's nae another ship in the neighborhood but ours and the ones in the dimensional fold. I see no reason for it to fire on those, or us."

"Nor do I," Gonzales said. "Are you certain they aren't simply testing their systems, running diagnostic checks?"

"I'm nae certain of a thing, because they've stopped talkin' to us. The ship won't answer our hails."

"Strange."

"And Chan'ya says the captain won't talk to her, either. But we know communications are passin' between this ship and that one. So somebody on the *Enterprise* is talkin' to somebody on the *Ton'bey*. If there's conversation, then someone ought to be able to order the *Ton'bey* to stand down."

Gonzales steepled his hands and touched his fingertips to his chin. "Mister Scott, Ixtoldans are very private people. Individually, they're uncomfortable with others asking them direct questions, or even making direct statements to them. You'll notice that they don't even have a pronoun for the first person singular. They exist, more or less, in a bubble of misdirection, making allusions, oftentimes very subtly, to important matters rather than addressing them outright. This personal characteristic is carried out on a societal level, as well. The Ixtoldan power structure is as antagonistic toward direct discussion as individuals are. It makes for . . . interesting diplomacy, let's say. Interesting, and difficult."

"I'm sure it does," Scotty said. "You make it sound like there's only one society. Are all Ixtoldan cultures the same?"

"Oddly enough, there is essentially only one society on the planet, at least one with any power or influence. Part of why we're traveling there is to make our own on-the-ground determination of the level of advancement of that society, and of how it came to be so homogeneous. So yes, effectively, there's just the one, and it operates as I've described. It is entirely possible that Chan'ya is in regular contact with the *Ton'bey*, but that since you asked her outright, she could not bring herself to admit it."

Scotty felt like his scalp was coming unglued and his brains beginning to leak out of his ears. "How should I have asked her, then?"

Gonzales closed his eyes for a moment, as if the answer might be inscribed on the insides of his eyelids. "Perhaps something like, 'If it were possible,

would Ixtoldans on board the *Enterprise* communicate with those on the *Ton'bey*? And if so, would those
on the *Enterprise* ever consider telling the *Ton'bey* to
power down its weapons?'"

"Acch," Scotty said. "I thought Captain Kirk had it
bad. But you, you've got to talk yourself into knots just
to do your job."

"It is often difficult," Gonzales admitted. "We have
to try to walk in the shoes of those we negotiate with,
metaphorically, of course. If we can't think like they
do, we can't figure out how best to achieve our own
desired results. But like an actor rehearsing a role,
sometimes we can get stuck in character, as it were."

"Well, if you've any influence over Minister
Chan'ya, you'd be doin' us all a service if you can get
her to make the *Ton'bey* stand down. I told its captain
that I'd blow the ship to bits if it tries to use those
weapons, and I meant it."

"I will see what I can do, Mister Scott."

"You'd better do it fast, too. Because if they decide
to use those weapons on us, at this range, we'll be
takin' heavy casualties. We won't be able to guarantee
anybody's safety. Including hers."

Twenty-two

Green beams sliced through the ship's dimly lit interior. Tikolo had only an instant's warning, but she dived behind a mound of debris. It wouldn't hold them off for long, but it gave her time to draw her phaser and try to suss out where her best targets were. She eyed the Romulans through gaps in the mounded furnishings and electronics equipment and who-knew-what else sheltering her.

She counted six of them. They knew where she had gone and focused their attentions there. Their disruptor beams churned through the rubble. It wouldn't protect her for long. As soon as she fired back, she would be a target again, and they would all know exactly where to aim.

The decision was being taken out of her hands, though, as her shield was being rapidly torn away. She sucked in a deep breath and made ready to jump and fire at the same moment.

Then red beams pierced the empty space to her left. Three Romulans fell immediately, and the remaining three returned fire, shooting toward the newcomers. Tikolo took advantage of the chance to shoot, taking down another Romulan. Someone behind her screamed and she heard a body thud to the deck. She shot a second Romulan, and someone else got the last of them.

"Greene's hit!" someone shouted. "Jamal!"

A huge, muscular, dark-haired man came into view from someplace behind Tikolo. "Are you okay, Miranda?"

One of the pretenders, those who acted like friends. She didn't know them, but they had fired on the Romulans, so her first instinct, that she was surrounded by hostiles, must have been mistaken. Now the question was, should she run, or play along?

"Miranda?" he said again. "They got Greene."

Another one joined the first. This one was a woman, tall and broad through the shoulders. She wore a red uniform much like Tikolo's. The man's shirt was red, but superficially similar as well. They had spared no effort to carry out their charade. The woman had tears glistening in her eyes and streaks carving through the dirt on her cheeks. "Where do you suppose they came from?" she asked. "Miranda, you said there were Romulans outside—how did you know?"

Tikolo could shoot them both where they stood. But there were others, just out of her field of view. One down; she couldn't remember how many that left. If they had gone to such lengths, even faking uniforms, to earn her trust, what was their ultimate goal? They could have shot her as easily, but none of them had raised a weapon toward her.

The petty officer shook her head and bit the inside of her cheek until she tasted blood. Her head was foggy, and she needed it clear. She had the nagging sensation that she knew something about these people, about their uniforms—and about her own. She could not imagine, for the moment, where she was or why she was in a uniform and carrying a weapon. It felt as natural as breathing, but what did that tell her? Was she a soldier in some army? And what was this bizarre place, with chunks of glowing stone providing scant illumination, dark passageways, walls furred with growth, and stacked detritus behind which one could take cover? She had known that Romulans were attacking, though until the woman had mentioned it, she had forgotten. How had she known?

Uncertainty swamped her. She didn't know whom to trust, and that included her own heart and mind. If these uniformed people weren't her allies, was she actually with the Romulans? How could she find out?

Another man stepped up beside the woman. He was handsome, in a way, his short hair thinning on top and brushed away from his face. His eyes were brown and soft, his chin hard, his cheeks carved by trenches. But the glowing rocks revealed blood on his hands and a smear of it on his forehead, where he must have touched himself. He looked both familiar and strange, like someone she had seen and remembered, but never actually known.

Yet he looked at her as if he knew her, and he came toward her, his bloody hands outstretched, with no fear or guile. "Miranda, you're okay. I was so worried."

She shrank away from his touch. Misunderstanding, he looked at his blood-soaked hands. "I'm sorry, Miranda. It's Jamal's. I couldn't save him—maybe if Doctor McCoy were here, but I don't think even he could have done much. Poor kid was so torn up."

"I . . ." Tikolo said. "I'm sorry, I don't understand."

"The Romulans shot him," the man said.

He didn't seem to view her as a threat, and they made no hostile moves toward her. Maybe they were friends, or even more than that. She could hardly imagine that if she knew these people, she wouldn't recognize them, recall their names. But even her own present circumstances, not to mention her past, were blanks, when she tried to examine them. Put that down to the intensity of the moment, the sudden firefight? Maybe. But still, since the fight had ended, those things hadn't returned.

She could remember darkness, solitude, terror, want.

That was all.

She decided, for the moment, to align herself with these people. She would remain alert, though. At the first sign of treachery, she would kill them all before they could kill her.

"I'm fine," she said. She had to pretend she knew them, which could be tricky since she couldn't even summon their names. She knew her own, Miranda Ang Tikolo, but no one else's. "Thanks for the help."

"Of course," the man said. He wiped his bloody hands on his pants and extended one of them toward her. Tikolo pushed aside any squeamishness and clasped it, letting him help her to her feet. When both were upright, he gave her a quick embrace, then let go as if he had embarrassed himself. "Sorry. Public place, right? Though it's not terribly public here, after all."

"It's okay," she said. Maybe she really did know these people. Maybe the man was a lover. She couldn't say for sure, either way. She obviously had not been born in these few moments, but had a past, associations, friendships. She had enough sense of herself to know what she looked like, and she had what seemed like vestigial memories of pleasure. She just couldn't reach down inside and find specifics—the who, the what, the when.

And the memories of pleasure, fractured as they were, were far outweighed by pain.

"Where to?" she asked.

"You're in charge," the man said.

"I'm . . . out of ideas."

"We need to keep looking for Captain Kirk and the others," he said.

"And hope there aren't any more Romulans around," the tall woman added.

"What about Greene?" the other man asked. "We can't just leave him."

"Bring him, then," Tikolo said. If she was in charge, she would make the decisions. As long as she didn't have to haul the corpse, she was fine with somebody else doing it. And the one who had asked looked big enough to carry almost anything.

She started off in the direction the Romulans had come from, figuring that, although she had no clue where they were going, at least they hadn't come from that way. They climbed the stairs, past the Romulan bodies, and kept going.

Spock spent his first minutes in the library familiarizing himself with Ixtoldan text. At a glance it looked like random scratches, mostly up and down, with slight ticks to the right and left. Every now and then there was a swirling shape that connected some of the scratches, and occasional shapes—mostly dots but also triangles and dashes that curved up or down—floated above and below.

His studies of Ixtoldan history and culture had included a few small samples of Ixtoldan writing, so it wasn't entirely unfamiliar. He dredged his memory and came up with enough data to get started learning what the basic shapes meant: how a scratch that leaned slightly to the left and included a short tick to the right, about two-thirds of the way up, differed from one that was essentially identical but leaning right. Ixtoldan writing was more alphabet than ideogram, so multiple characters had to be strung together to form words, and words to form sentences. Though he saw little punctuation at first, as he got deeper into it he realized that the curved dashes and dots were, in fact, punctuation marks.

He perused some of the physical books he found lying about the library, which was better preserved than most of the ship, and before long he was reading and comprehending. The first books he tried were simple technical manuals detailing some of the huge ship's systems, and held little interest except as tools for learning the language.

The data storage media and computers would be useless without full power to the ship's systems. One of the books might yet tell him how to accomplish that, though he doubted he could do it alone, with the materials at hand. Especially not inside the fold, where the effects might be considerably different than those expected or desired.

No, he would have to confine his studies to the physical books. It would not have been his preference, all else being equal, but it was the only logical approach, given the circumstances.

But where to begin? That was the quandary. There were probably a hundred books. Few if any were mass-produced. Most were bound in something like animal hide, with no text on the covers or spines to identify their contents.

As Spock stood looking at the shelves and trying to formulate a plan, he felt the presence again. Its familiar warmth told him it was the same one that had led him into this room in the first place. He was, once again, overtaken by a sensation of welcoming, of peaceful acceptance, that cut through his Vulcan side to the humanity he declined to embrace.

"Hello again," he said. The Vulcan felt foolish speaking to empty air, but he didn't know if the noncorporeal being could hear. If she could—and once again, he had the distinct impression that *it* was a *she,* and he wondered if that was why she touched his human side, his mother's genetic contribution, so easily—then she would expect him to speak. If she couldn't hear, then it wouldn't bother her that he did. "Do you have something further to show me?"

The presence responded with a gentle tug on his hand. Spock allowed himself to be led across the room, to a particular bookcase. They stopped before it, and his hand was placed on the upper corner of the spine of a particular volume, on the third shelf from the top. At first glance, it was in no way distinct from those around it. He pulled it from the shelf and opened it. It had been handwritten in something like a dark, soft-leaded pencil. The script was more flowing than what he had seen in the technical manuals. "Is this . . . yours?" he asked. "Did you write this?"

An unspoken affirmation wrapped around him like the gentlest of hugs.

"Very well, then," he said. He took his seat again, and sat down to begin reading.

Twenty-three

Captain Kirk led the way through a huge double doorway. The right-hand door had been removed in what looked like a violent fashion, leaving bent, splintered steel where it was hinged. The other door had suffered a different sort of damage, although not necessarily unrelated, resulting in a large bulge on the outer surface. He hoped that whatever had broken the doors would not make a reappearance. The invisible attack on Gao and a few Romulans notwithstanding, he hadn't seen much that was truly dangerous on this ship. All he wanted was to collect the rest of his crew and put this ship behind them.

The doorway led into what appeared to be a vast storeroom. Around the sides were multiple galleries, connected by ladders that had, in most cases, collapsed. The center was open to the ceiling, which must have been sixty feet high. Shelving units, some of which had fallen down and taken out others, like giant dominos, filled the big central area. Crates were stacked against the walls; these, too, had shifted and fallen over and been torn apart by violent force. The light from the inset stones didn't reach all the way up, so he couldn't see what was on the upper galleries that ringed the big space. The floor was an obstacle course of fallen detritus.

"Bunker!" he cried. "Tikolo! Chandler! Is anybody in here?"

His voice bounced around the space, returning in the form of faint echoes. No other voices answered his call.

"They're not here," McCoy said.

"I don't see any way around," Kirk said. "If we want to get to the other side, we have to go through."

"I don't like it."

"Fortunately," Kirk whispered to the doctor, "liking anything on this vessel is not required. All we have to do is survive it."

"Aren't you usually the optimistic one, Jim?"

"I am optimistic, Bones. I am certain that at least one of us will make it off this ship alive. Maybe not in one piece, but alive."

McCoy *humph*ed. "I guess you're more optimistic than me, at that. I'm no longer so sure of anything."

The ship gave a jolt. Kirk froze, bracing for the worst. But nothing happened, that he could determine.

"Now I'm really confused," Kirk said. "I thought we'd all change into clowns, or suddenly find ourselves on twenty-first-century Mars, or something." He eyed McCoy closely. "Maybe only you changed."

McCoy's hands flew to his face. "What?" he asked.

Kirk chuckled. As they had talked, they'd moved deeper into the storeroom. Most of what remained on the shelving structures was indecipherable, covered as it was by a thick layer of the same growth that coated most of the ship's surfaces. Some were recognizably cartons, but made of what material and containing what, he had no idea.

"A storeroom this size tells me one thing," Romer said.

"What's that?" Beachwood asked.

"This ship was intended for a very long space voyage."

"You're probably right," Kirk said. "They weren't counting on being able to resupply any time soon."

"That means somewhere there are food stores," Beachwood said. "I don't mind telling you, I'm getting a little hungry."

"I'm sure we'll find the others soon," Kirk said. "This is a big vessel, but we've managed to cover a lot of ground." His own natural optimism notwithstanding, the captain was aware as he said it that he was trying to put the best face on things. It was entirely possible that the ship had no fixed dimensions at all, and that they could explore for the rest of eternity without seeing all of it. He had told McCoy the truth: he still believed somebody would make it back to the *Enterprise*. Who it would be, he couldn't have said. And he was beginning to doubt, more and more, that Gao would be the only casualty. There were forces at work on the ship that he couldn't comprehend, and it was hard to fight against the unknown.

Would it have been better to admit his fears to the doctor? Should he take advantage of the momentary calm to tell McCoy good-bye, to say that he had never served with a better officer or a better friend? Should he go back up to say the same to Spock?

Saying any of it out loud would have been counterproductive, he decided, so Kirk kept it to himself. Drawing people's attention to things they could not control would do no good, and admitting defeat ran counter to every instinct he had. The captain hoped the next few minutes would bring about a reunion with the rest of the *Enterprise* crew and all his fears would prove unfounded.

They walked down a wide central aisle, flanked on both sides by shelving units that reached toward the unseen heights. Near what Kirk took to be the middle of the room, they came across a large clearing, though whether it had been planned or the structures had simply fallen away, he couldn't say. The floor was relatively smooth and clear in its center, and he was just thinking that it would make for easier going when something sailed into view from one of the upper galleries. It landed on the hard floor, bounced twice, and came to rest.

The object was so out of place that even though he recognized it, he couldn't react for the first few tenths of a second. Then his head cleared, and he shouted, "Bomb! Take cover!"

His crew members scrambled, everyone seeking the strongest nearby object to duck behind. He did the same thing, but he was out in front and knew he had to get some distance between himself and the Romulan explosive device.

As he ran, he noticed that at the far end of the room—the end through which they had entered—the doorway appeared completely sealed off. But that was impossible, because only one of the doors, and the wreckage of the other, had been in place.

Then he quit distracting himself with thoughts of what was or was not possible. He hurled himself to the deck behind a couple of fallen shelving units, and hoped that their structural integrity, combined with whatever goods they still held, would shield him.

He had barely touched down when the bomb exploded.

A brilliant light filled the space, searing outlines of thousands of shelves and possibly millions of cartons, into Kirk's head. That was followed by a powerful concussion wave that carried dirt and shreds of whatever had been closest to the blast, metal pellets that tore into softer matter like old-fashioned bullets and bits of packing material and other, unknown objects. Although he was behind the tumbled-down shelving units, some of that still found Kirk, lacerating his flesh and tearing his uniform. Behind that wave came the heat, intense and seeming to linger, and the sound, which filled his ears and left them ringing. Through that, though, he could hear the cries of the injured and the clatter of everything that had been blown into the air coming down again, as the ship's artificial gravity dictated that it must.

"Stay sharp!" Kirk shouted. "The Romulans are next!"

He had barely got the words out when they attacked.

Disruptor rifles fired from the upper elevations, all around them. "We're surrounded!" Beachwood cried.

"Fire at will!" Kirk said. "We're Starfleet, damn it!"

The sentiment would doubtless have been lost on the Romulans, but he thought it might mean something to his people. Phasers sent brilliant pulses toward the unseen Romulans. Kirk took grim satisfaction in the scream of one, followed by the unmistakable sound of a body falling from a height. Kirk waited until he saw another disruptor weapon's beam, and fired at its source. He heard only a faint thump, but that weapon didn't fire again.

The Romulans had several clear advantages. They had elevation, and at every stage of military history, firing down at an enemy had been easier than firing up. They could back away from the edges of the upper galleries, which shielded them from the Starfleet phasers. They encircled the Starfleet crew, which meant they could fire from any angle. They had darkness, while the glowing stones cast light on the lower level. Their numbers were unknown, as was their motivation.

That last, though, Kirk could guess at. They were a warlike race in general, and they had no love for the Federation, or the Starfleet personnel who enforced their exile to the region beyond the Neutral Zone. They had tested the willingness of Starfleet to compel their compliance before, and nobody believed they wouldn't do it again.

There were, however, some things that Kirk couldn't figure out. How had they come so far from the Neutral Zone? And why attack inside the dimensional fold? How had they slipped past the *Enterprise* and the *Ton'bey*? These questions had plagued him since that first brief skirmish, and he had found no answers yet. Maybe they could take some Romulans alive and question them.

That was a consideration for later, though. To worry about taking prisoners, they first had to survive the onslaught. As much as it did Kirk's heart good to hear the sounds of Romulans falling, he couldn't ignore the pained screams of his own people.

He had to try to get around, to see who was hit, and how bad their injuries were.

He rose to a crouch. A disruptor beam angled toward him from high above. He dodged it and fired back. He thought he heard a grunt of pain, but couldn't be certain.

"Who's hit?" he called. "Anybody?"

"Beachwood is," Romer said. Kirk barely recognized her voice. He shook his head, but that didn't help with the ringing. "I'm over here with him."

"Anybody else?"

He heard a moan, close by. "Who's that?" he asked.

Another moan answered him. Someone to his left fired a phaser at an eighty-degree angle. A disruptor beam fired back, briefly, then stopped abruptly.

Kirk moved again, toward where he had heard the moans. Another form got there first. "I've got it, Jim," McCoy said. "It's Jensen."

"Is he—?"

"It's not good."

Then a voice rang out, loud and clear, echoing in the big space. A Romulan voice. "Starfleet! A word!"

"I am Captain James T. Kirk, of the *Starship Enterprise*," Kirk replied. "You have acted aggressively, without reason or quarter. I must insist that you cease all hostilities and hold a conference with me."

"I am afraid you are in no position to insist upon anything, Captain," the Romulan said. "But I am prepared to accept your surrender."

"You'll be waitin' a long time for that, you no-good—"

Kirk cut McCoy off. "Never mind that, Bones. Tend to Jensen." He raised his voice again. "Whom am I addressing?"

"Your choice is very simple, Captain Kirk," the Romulan said, ignoring the question. Kirk listened closely, trying, to the extent of his abilities in the echoing space, with his ears still ringing from the initial blast, to locate the speaker. "Surrender, or die."

"What if I want a third option?"

"What you want does not enter—"

Kirk raised his phaser and loosed a burst at the unseen speaker. The Romulan's sentence came to an abrupt end, punctuated by a sharp groan and a heavy *thump*.

"We're winning," Kirk said.

"You've got a strange idea of victory," McCoy answered.

"They wouldn't have asked for our surrender if we weren't beating them, Bones. There probably aren't many of them left."

"Captain?" Another voice issued from the darkness, but this time at ground level, and slightly behind Kirk.

"Is that you, Mister O'Meara?"

"Yes, sir." O'Meara came closer, stooped low, pushing through the debris covering the deck. In the faint light, Kirk could see that he'd suffered a cut above his left eye, but otherwise seemed to be uninjured.

No Romulans fired at him as he approached, which Kirk took as validation of his theory. The one who had demanded surrender might have been the only one remaining. "What is it?" he asked.

"It's . . . this whole attack, sir. There's something strange about it."

"There's been something strange about every moment we've spent on this ship," Kirk replied. He took
another look back at the double doors through which
they had entered, which had appeared whole right before the bomb went off. Now the right-hand one—on
his left, from this vantage point—had been torn off at
the hinge. Through the darkness, he couldn't tell for
sure, but he was willing to bet that the other one was
dented on this side, bulging on the other. Somehow,
they had come through the doors after the blast had
damaged them, then suffered through the blast itself.
He didn't want to think about the physics of it. That,
he was convinced, would only lead to madness.

"Yes, sir, that's true. But this—the specifics of this
attack—I've seen this before."

"Explain," Kirk said.

"Okay, not *seen,* exactly. Except in my mind's eye.
But I've heard about it."

"I'm not following you, O'Meara."

"I'm not describing this well," O'Meara said. "I'm
sorry. It's all a little disconcerting. But . . . I guess I
should start by telling you that I am deeply, unre-
servedly in love with Miranda Tikolo. Petty Officer
Tikolo."

"I know who she is."

"Of course you do, sir, sorry."

"And I hope you don't think that fact has escaped
the notice of anyone on the crew."

"Really, sir? I mean, I guess I'm not surprised. I'm

probably not as discreet as I ought to be. But I do have to disagree with you on one point—I think it has escaped Miranda's notice. At least, she doesn't seem to let it affect her."

"Your point being?"

"Captain, my point is, she has described this whole attack to me."

"Say that again?"

O'Meara hesitated. Kirk could almost see him trying to formulate a rational sentence. "All of it, sir. Starfleet personnel down below, in this huge warehouse-type space. The darkness. The messed-up doors. Then a Romulan bomb comes bouncing in out of nowhere. It goes off, and there's a firefight. Romulans shooting down from above, Starfleet trying to return fire, but at a tactical disadvantage."

"But that never happened to her," Kirk said. "She wasn't even on the outpost when the Romulans attacked. And they never left their ship. They vaporized the outposts with the ship's weapons. There was no close combat."

"You're right, sir," O'Meara said. "I should have been clearer. When she tells me about it, she's telling me about a dream she has. She's on the outpost, and the Romulans land, and there's a battle. She has this nightmare again and again."

"How does it end, man?" someone else asked.

"She always wakes up before it's over. Or that's what she tells me. It's a nightmare, terrifying for her, and when she recognizes that she's dreaming, she says she claws herself back to wakefulness."

"I guess it's not impossible that she could dream about a similar situation," Kirk said. He eyed the upper reaches, but nobody fired down upon them.

"It's not similar, Jim," McCoy said. "It's identical."

"Bones?"

"She's told me about the same nightmare. In our therapy sessions. One morning, she was in bad shape, clearly hadn't had enough sleep. I asked her about her dreams, and she told me this one. Same thing she told Mister O'Meara. I asked for details. Since then, when the dream recurs, she lets me know. This whole setup felt familiar to me, but I didn't know why until O'Meara said something."

"So you both are trying to tell me that Miranda Tikolo dreamed this exact firefight."

"Yes," O'Meara said.

"I can't explain it, Jim," McCoy said. "But it's the truth."

"She's not even here."

"That doesn't seem to be a factor," McCoy said.

"It's just not—"

"What, Jim? Not possible? You want to think twice before you make that claim, given where we are."

"Point granted, Bones. Still, I don't get it."

"Maybe there's nothing to get," McCoy said. "This damn ship is bouncing around through dimensions, through universes, playing hell with reality as we know it. I couldn't begin to imagine the mechanism, but somehow it's manifesting people and places that those of us on board have known."

"That's possible, I suppose," Kirk admitted. "I mean, I don't know *how* it's possible, but I can't argue that it isn't." He was thinking about his uncle Frank, who had been there earlier, so clearly visible, present even down to his scent. And the green-tinged landscape that Romer had recognized. Those things had to come from somewhere.

"Jim, the laws of physics are meaningless here, we know that. That doesn't mean that there aren't some kind of laws at work, which we don't understand. The universe has order to it, or at least we like to think so. And maybe there's even order here, only we haven't recognized it yet."

"Okay, say that's true. Where does it get us?"

"What if part of the order here is that the things that are manifested all come from someplace? Or from somebody? What if overwhelmingly strong emotional states can, in essence, create their own reality?"

Kirk considered the idea. No Romulan had fired at them in several minutes. As if—as if the sleeper whose dream had created them had never slept beyond that point. "Go on."

"These Romulans were here. Literally, physically here. But they were here because they were created from, I don't know, let's say the stuff of chaos, by Tiko-lo's mind. I mean, we've all got thoughts, fears hurtling through our subconscious minds, but hers are more pronounced, maybe. They overwhelm everybody else's more mundane emotions. And as she interacts with them and becomes more frightened—"

"The manifestations become more widespread. Yes, I guess that's possible. But the injured—"

"And the dead, Jim. We lost Jensen, a few minutes ago."

"Beachwood?" Kirk called out.

"He's hurt, but he'll live," Romer said.

"Good."

"Anyway," McCoy went on, "yes, Jensen is really dead, and Beachwood is really wounded. The Romulans were *real*. They didn't come here in a starship, though, and unless we can get Tikolo calmed down, I'd bet we haven't seen the last of them."

"I can do that," O'Meara said. "If we can find her, I can calm her down. If she's manifesting these guys because she's in a distraught mental state, I can help."

"This is all still very much theoretical," Kirk said.

"I understand that, sir. But we need to find her, anyway. And the others."

"Suggestions?" Kirk said.

"Let me talk to her," O'Meara offered. "If she's living through this same thing, being chased around this ship by Romulan soldiers, she might be pretty manic."

"He's right about that, Jim," McCoy said. "Fear of Romulans is a continuing stressor for her."

"If I can get close to her, I can reach her. She trusts

me, as much as she can trust anyone right now. I believe that. I know I can bring her around."

"It's worth a shot. And the immediate danger seems to be over," Kirk said. "Can Beachwood travel?"

"Aye, sir," Beachwood said. His voice was weak, but his determination shone through.

"Good. We'll come back for Jensen." Kirk knew that meant two bodies to pick up later, but they couldn't be slowed by bringing them along. And Jensen was among their heaviest; it would take two to carry him. "Let's go, people. Let's get this over and done with."

Twenty-four

Minister Chan'ya stood at the head of the table in her quarters. The others were seated around it, which she liked because that was the only time she was the tallest. Height did not always equal power on Ixtolde, but there was an undeniable correlation. She had achieved considerable influence on her home planet, but had she been taller, there would have been fewer limits on her potential accomplishments.

Well, she could still achieve things others didn't dare to dream of. But first she had to negotiate the current crisis. "They have been on the ship far too long," she said.

"We agree," Keneseth said. Chan'ya spun toward him, but stopped herself before she blasted his presumptuousness. She did not in the least care that he agreed. The only reason he was here was that his mother had great social standing back home, and the ears of several important Ixtoldans.

"Yes," Chan'ya said, as pleasantly as she could manage. "We are all in agreement. Who can say what they might have learned in this time? Their presence there was a danger to us, and now that danger has become transferred to their return here. Should they make it safely back to the *Enterprise,* all our efforts at winning Federation membership will have been in vain."

"But how can their return be prevented, Minister?" Cris'ya asked. She picked at a scab on her cheek with the same clawed finger with which she had probably created it.

"That is our greatest difficulty," Chan'ya said. "We seem to have run out of good options. If we take action—which means destroying the ship and everyone on board—we will lose any chance at Federation membership. We will also, in every likelihood, be subject to disciplinary measures levied by the Federation. We should hate to spend any more time than necessary on Earth, and we have no desire to experience the inside of a Federation prison."

"But if we don't," Skanderen observed, "then Kirk and the others come back. And report what they saw. Which means—"

"Which means, no Federation membership," Chan'ya replied. "And instead, we will face disciplinary measures from our own. And they will, we are sure, be every bit as harsh."

"More so," Cris'ya said. "The peoples of the Federation are soft. They rely on numbers and on the advantages granted them by commerce to do what we would do by force of will."

"We are in agreement," Chan'ya told her. "But do not discount the power of commerce. That, all along, has been our reason for seeking Federation membership. Ixtolde is richer than . . . than what we had before, but she is far from rich. She will not support us all for much longer, not without trade."

Trade was Tre'aln's area of expertise, and he spoke up. "Chan'ya speaks wisdom. Putting our trade prospects in jeopardy is unthinkable."

Chan'ya took her seat again. This whole situation had been wearying, and it was far from over. "And yet, we have no choice. Jeopardy exists either way. Act and face the consequences. Or don't act, and face what might be greater consequences still."

"Have you reached a decision, then?" Tre'aln asked. "Because we believe something must be done."

"We see only one possible solution," Chan'ya said. She placed her palms flat on the table. "The *Ton'bey* must destroy the ship before the captain and his party can escape it."

Cris'ya's golden eyes went wide. "But then—"

"Then," Chan'ya interrupted, "we declare that the captain of the *Ton'bey* acted against our express commands. We punish him twice as severely as the Federation would have. Only by placing all blame squarely on him can we hope to salvage anything from this mission. And the cost of failure is not one that we are prepared to pay."

"Then it is agreed," Tre'aln said.

Chan'ya looked around the table, at each in turn. Cris'ya, Skanderen, the so-far-silent Antelis, and finally Keneseth. "It is agreed," each one said.

"Well and good," Chan'ya said when they had reached consensus. "Keneseth, tell that captain what must be done. And do it quickly; we fear the *Enterprise* crew is trying to monitor our communications. This one, they must not intercept."

"Your name," Spock said, "is Aleshia."

He felt the warmth on his shoulders that he could interpret only as affirmation.

"The journal you had me read. It is yours. Your story, your life."

And there it was again. It was, he had to admit, a pleasant sensation.

"You came onto this ship from Ixtolde. You were an original Ixtoldan."

Once more, that comforting weight.

"I . . . could not read all of it," Spock admitted. "Your language is foreign to me, as is your form of writing. I made progress, but there was some that I missed. Yet, I should like to know more."

That elicited no response. He did not interpret that as opposition, but instead as acceptance. He held his right hand up at about the height of his own head. "Come before me," he said. "Right here, to my hand."

What he was about to try was risky in the extreme. It was rarely attempted, even by the most practiced Vulcans. But it was not, he knew, impossible. Not impossible to do, not impossible to survive. He had to cling to that knowledge or chance frightening himself out of trying it. If he didn't believe, fully, that he could do it, then he would fail.

Failure would be disastrous.

Failure, in this place, in this situation, he might not survive.

"I need to touch you," Spock said. "I am aware, of course, that you have no physical form. Nevertheless, I can sense your presence. You feel to me as a slight warmth, the very lightest weight imaginable. Perhaps those things are imaginary, existing only in my mind and not in the world of material things. Just the same, I need to be in contact with you." He twitched his fingers. "Just here, please."

After a moment, he felt the trace warmth, as if a hand had just touched his palm glancingly and then moved away. But the warmth lingered.

"Thank you, Aleshia," Spock said. "What I am about to do is a curiously intimate thing. We call it a Vulcan mind-meld. It has not always been accepted, even among my kind, because it can be seen as invasive. I believe that is inaccurate, though. It would be invasive if one of us were to do it to the other. Instead, each of us would be doing it *with* the other. It is more a sharing than an intrusion. Just the same, you may find it strange, even frightening, at first."

He did not tell her how frightening it was to him. Such destructive emotions had to be shut down, and his Vulcan psycho-suppression training would allow him to do that. Any element of risk had to be forgotten. This was a somewhat unusual circumstance, but he was convinced that Aleshia had a mind, and any being with a mind could be melded with.

Or so Spock chose to believe.

The thought came to him, briefly, that although Aleshia had consciousness, hers was linked with the others on the ship, part of the group-mind.

Melding with Aleshia might mean melding with that group-mind.

And its madness might be transferable. Contagious. There was no better way to catch insanity than opening one's mind to it.

Again, thoughts like that had to be suppressed. He could not afford to accept the possibility of danger, or failure, or madness. He had to deny those ideas any foothold, or he should not even attempt this.

But he had no choice. He had read Aleshia's journal. It had been enlightening, to say the least.

Now he had to *understand*.

"Are you ready, Aleshia?"

He still felt that trace of warmth against his palm, but at the same time he felt it on his shoulders. Her way of saying "Yes."

"Then," Spock said. "Let us begin . . ."

They met another group of Romulans on the next deck down. O'Meara was out in front, Kirk keeping a close eye on him to make sure his concern for Tikolo didn't outweigh caution.

The last few encounters had altered the mood of the team. There had been an urgency to find the others and get off the ship, but doing so had seemed to be low-risk. Nobody liked it there, but until the attack on Gao, and then the Romulan skirmishes, danger had seemed like a remote possibility. Now everybody knew it literally could lurk around any corner. Easy banter was gone; instead, they moved swiftly and quietly, weapons drawn and moods bleak.

So far, no one had suggested abandoning the missing crew members. The captain didn't think anyone would. Certainly not to his face, because everyone in his crew knew what his reaction to such a proposal would be. But although it was possible that some were thinking it, no one who would say it aloud would find a welcome on *Enterprise*. Kirk couldn't know every member of the crew before they were assigned to his ship, but once they were there he tried to gauge each one according to how well he or she lived up to the ideals that Starfleet promoted. He wanted people who possessed personal courage, who were willing to put the interests of the whole team above their own, and who would watch one another's backs as closely as their own. Some didn't meet that standard, and when he discovered that, he did his best to either turn them around or transfer them off the ship.

The captain trusted those who had volunteered for

this mission, and he would do everything in his power to get them back to the *Enterprise* alive. But that niggling doubt, that sensation that the conditions existing within the fold made this mission far more dangerous than anticipated, wouldn't go away. He was not, he knew, superhuman. He was just a man, and men sometimes failed.

Kirk pushed those thoughts into a metaphorical mental box and closed the lid. They were self-destructive, and he had no time for them. Later, if need be, he could take them out and examine them. For now, they were distracting him from the more important task of studying his surroundings.

This deck looked more like a typical starship's than the warehouse-style one above it. A narrow, utilitarian corridor was lined with doors along one side, leading into various engineering areas. Kirk was convinced they were getting close to the lowest decks. The possibility existed that Tikolo and the others had gone back up, by a different route, and were waiting around the upper decks wondering where everyone had gone. But Spock was up there—aware, Kirk hoped, of the Romulan threat—so if Tikolo's team found him they would stay close, knowing that reunion would come soon. Kirk worried about Spock, alone on this menace of a ship, but his first officer had proven himself hard to outflank. If he had to leave one member of the crew alone, Spock would be his first choice.

O'Meara had opened a door that led into a warren

of machinery, huge, primitive things that Kirk, looking over the security officer's shoulder, surmised had once provided propulsion and an artificial atmosphere. "This stuff looks ancient," Kirk said. "Earth passed this sort of technology by 2120 or thereabouts."

"Yes, sir," O'Meara agreed. "On the other hand, anybody could service it with a big enough wrench and maybe a hammer. Convenient for a long trip, in case the engineers don't survive."

He had been about to close the door again when Kirk heard a soft, clanking noise deep in the room's bowels. "Shh!" the captain ordered. O'Meara froze. A moment later, the noise repeated, joined by the low murmur of conversation.

"It's them," O'Meara whispered.

"Not necessarily," Kirk countered. He summoned the others from the hallway and explained. In a moment, they were moving silently through the big room in small groups, each one taking a different aisle through the machinery.

The room had gone absolutely silent. Kirk thought the first noise he'd heard had been someone walking through the aisles and bumping into the machinery. Chances were that, quiet as they had been, someone had heard the *Enterprise* crew coming in, and the listeners had gone to ground and were waiting for an ambush opportunity. The captain had conceded that advantage by dividing his team, but he had to balance caution and the necessity for finding his missing people. If in fact the noise had been made by Tikolo and her squad, then no harm done. If it was more Romulans, then they would be ready for battle.

Romer's voice shattered the silence. "Here!" she cried. The sound of phasers firing followed, then the slightly different pitch of disruptor rifles returning fire, and the crackle of shots going astray.

The others converged on that aisle. Kirk went over the machines instead of around, and from that vantage point spotted half a dozen Romulan soldiers taking cover behind a bank of heavy equipment. He had an angle that allowed him to shoot over the top of their shelter, and he used it. Two Romulans fell quickly, but then he had to dive from his perch, because it also gave them an easy shot at him. Disruptor rays blasted where he had just been, tearing metal and sending sparks flying.

He touched down in the aisle that Romer and McCoy had been in from the start. The others had joined them, and from behind their own covered positions, were blasting away at the Romulans.

He tapped Beachwood and O'Meara and motioned toward the left. They understood, and followed him underneath a bank of machinery, then around the end of the next row. From there they worked their way quietly past the Romulans and cut over again.

The Romulans were still engaged with the Starfleet crew when Kirk once again climbed up on banks of machinery. When the other two crew members were in position, he shouted. "Hey, you guys! Up here!"

Two of the Romulans spun around. Kirk's first shot took one in the chest. He ducked return fire, then Beachwood got the second. The last two Romulans tried to break and run, but were cut down by fire from the main Starfleet group.

With the fight over, Kirk, Beachwood, and O'Meara rejoined the main group. O'Meara called out Tikolo's name, and Kirk let him, knowing that the shout would draw in any remaining Romulans.

"Is that wise?" said a deep voice from close by.

"Mister Spock, is that you?"

"It is indeed."

Kirk went around the end of the equipment bank and saw Spock walking toward them. "I thought you were supposed to stay put."

"I was," Spock said. "But I learned something that I thought you should know. Since you did not appear to be returning in a timely fashion, I decided to find you."

"Glad that you did that. If you could find Tikolo's group, and Bunker, as easily, we could get off this ship."

Twenty-five

"The passengers on this ship," Spock said as they continued their quest, "were the real Ixtoldans." He, Kirk, and McCoy spoke in low tones. The captain would decide what part of Spock's news, if any, to share with the rest of the crew.

"Define 'real,' please," Kirk said.

"Original."

"There are original and nonoriginal Ixtoldans?"

"Indeed there are, Captain. Those we think of as Ixtoldans—including Chan'ya and her retinue—came to Ixtolde from another planet in their system, which had been known previously as Ixtolde VII. And they did not come as friends."

Kirk opened a door and glanced inside, but it led only to a small storeroom, the contents of which were scattered all over the floor. "Are you saying they invaded Ixtolde?"

"Not at first, but eventually. First they came as trading partners. Ixtolde VII was far more technologically advanced than Ixtolde, whose inhabitants were, shall we say, technologically naive. They were a bucolic people, although there were a few cities of moderate size. Ix-tolde VII had wealth and the capability for interplanetary travel. But their planet was far from the system's sun. Scientists there had discovered forces at work that would move their world into an orbit that would cool it further, making it uninhabitable. Already, they could no longer sustain an indigenous agriculture. Working through agents in Ixtoldan cities, they arranged to buy huge quantities of Ixtolde's surplus of crops and livestock, and for a time, that satisfied their needs."

"For a time."

"Eventually, however, the residents of Ixtolde VII knew that their planet was unsustainable. They needed a new world, and they decided that the planet that had been their breadbasket would be the ideal place. Except for one minor inconvenience."

"Let me guess," McCoy said. "The planet's original population was in their way."

"You are correct, Doctor. The leaders of Ixtolde VII had two goals, which they did not believe were mutually exclusive. They were developing the technology that would allow them interstellar travel, but their planet was dying. They wanted a new home, and they wanted one of the primary benefits of interstellar capability."

"Federation membership?" Kirk suggested.

"Yes. It must be granted that the planet's leadership was forward-thinking. The Federation would not look kindly upon a race that attacked another planet and slaughtered or enslaved its populace."

Kirk shook his head. "That's an understatement, Mister Spock."

Around them, the rest of the team kept checking doors as the party kept moving forward. They always came back empty-handed. Kirk was beginning to wonder if the missing crew members had somehow left the ship.

"But they had a plan," Spock said. "They would invade in stages. At first, no one on Ixtolde knew what was happening to them. Aleshia says—"

"Aleshia?" Kirk asked.

"The woman who shared this knowledge with me."

"Now there's a woman?" McCoy asked. "Funny you didn't mention this right off the bat."

"Aleshia is noncorporeal," Spock explained. "But quite impressive, just the same. She told me that the first assaults came in the form of aerial shelling. She and her fellow villagers believed they were under attack by giants, because their legends included stories about malevolent giants storming around the countryside, crushing everything in their path."

"And they weren't technologically sophisticated enough to know the truth?"

"No. Giants fit into their belief set. Interplanetary war did not. And after the giant attacks came the acid rains."

"Not an uncommon phenomenon," Kirk said, "but usually one connected to an advanced technology with poor pollutant controls."

"This acid was not merely destructive," Spock said. "It was deadly. Aleshia still is unsure how it was accomplished, but I believe it could have been done fairly simply, through appropriate cloud seeding. Its effects were short-lived, so the planet's soil and livestock stores could be easily renewed. In fact—"

"Spare us the details," McCoy said.

"Very well, Doctor." Spock watched as another room was cleared. "The next stage involved actual contact, for the first time. Ixtolde VII sent ships to the surface to round up those who had survived thus far. They were taken to a central processing facility, and loaded onto this ship. Aleshia learned the healing arts, from the writings of a village wise woman named Margyan, and she did her best, within her limited means, to keep the ship's population healthy."

"Why didn't the invaders simply kill them?" Kirk asked.

"As far as they were concerned, they were merely doing what had to be done to preserve their own population. They did not consider themselves evil, and they were not conquering just for conquest. They wanted only to clear away any impediment to their settlement of Ixtolde. This was not the typical genocide, which is often marked by race hatred and includes such atrocities as widespread rape. None of that happened here. Instead, this killing had been coldly calculating: the simplest way to take over the planet was to drastically reduce the number of inhabitants, to eliminate any possibility of planetary self-defense. By launching the survivors into deep space on a century ship, built to carry them for generations, instead of killing every last one of them, they were able to assuage any guilt. They told themselves that they were only displacing the Ixtoldans, and that the ship would keep their race alive for centuries, until they found a new home and established themselves there."

"So banishment to a spacebound prison vessel was supposed to make them feel good about what they'd done?" McCoy asked, horrified.

"I am not justifying their actions, Doctor, merely explaining them as Aleshia explained them to me."

"How did she communicate all this, Spock?" Kirk asked. "Since she is, as you say, noncorporeal?"

"Through her writings, largely. She has put together a fairly substantial history of the entire affair. The rest came through a mind-meld."

"You melded with a being who has no physical form? Wasn't that dangerous?"

"Her lack of material substance was less dangerous, I believe, than the fact that she is part of the energy that makes up this ship's group-mind. And as Doctor McCoy correctly put it, that mind is insane. However, the mind-meld was successful, and Aleshia's personality, her presence, is strong enough that she was able to shield me."

"Sounds like you made quite the connection," McCoy said. "When are you gonna introduce us?"

Spock ignored the gibe. "The journey did not work out as planned," he said. "Instead of traveling through space for generations, the ship entered the dimensional fold and became trapped here. As we know, time and space in here are not what they are elsewhere. On the planet Ixtolde, a few generations have passed, and the invaders are firmly established as the sole inhabitants of the planet. Here on the ship, however, thousands of years have passed. More to the point, those years have passed in a chaotically random fashion characteristic of the dimensional fold. What we have encountered over the last several hours, the Ixtoldans have been dealing with for centuries. They have long since died, but due to some property of the fold I have not had a chance to explore, death is not final here. Electrical impulses remain. As we speculated, those impulses have organized into something we would call a group-mind. That group-mind is insane. The ship is not safe; all others who wander into the fold, such as the crew of the *McRaven*, find themselves drawn here and destroyed, either by dangers existing on the ship or by those manifesting from their own subconscious minds. Aleshia was one of the last to die; she was able to watch and record the whole unpleasant process."

"We need to get out of here," Kirk said.

"The longer we are here, the fewer of us there will be," Spock replied. "We will all die. The calculation is as simple as that."

"How much time do we have?" Kirk asked.

"That cannot be determined with any specificity. We might already have reached that point."

"Can't this girl help?" McCoy asked.

"Aleshia, Doctor. She already has. She has shared knowledge, and knowledge, as they say, is power."

"At this point," McCoy countered, "all knowledge is gonna do is make sure we die informed instead of ignorant."

"Then," Kirk said, "we'll just have to make sure we don't die."

"You got any foolproof ways around it, Jim?"

"I only know one way, Bones. Living."

During a period of relative calm, Miranda Tikolo had learned the names of the people she moved through the ship with, and what their intended destination was. The tall woman was Eve Chandler, the big man was Cesar Ruiz, and the one who seemed to be her lover was Stanley Vandella. Jamal Greene was the one who had died. They were looking for a Captain Kirk, whom they had left on one of the upper decks when they followed someone named Bunker.

She gleaned most of it through carefully phrased questions that didn't let on—she hoped—how ignorant she was about her situation. Some came from her own memories, which occasionally reflected back at her, like shards of a broken mirror catching the beam of a flashlight as it plays around a darkened room. Tikolo no longer had to wonder if she had been with these others. They were Starfleet, and so was she. Their enemies were the Romulans who were scattered about the ship they seemed to be trapped inside.

Those things she remembered now, or had pieced together. What she couldn't remember was everything that had preceded their arrival here. She didn't know where they were, what starship she was assigned to, or what the mission was.

Details could wait. What was important at the moment was survival, and then finding this Captain Kirk. Once her safety was assured, she could worry about the rest.

She was climbing a ladder, and was almost up to a small hatchway when the attack came.

Ruiz was behind her. Chandler and Vandella had already gone through, and Vandella was looking down through the opening, lowering a hand to help her up. She wondered how she ever could have put up with a man so solicitous, as if she couldn't be trusted to even climb a ladder unaided. She was fit, she was strong, and in spite of her momentary memory lapse, she was certain that she was mentally capable as well. Tikolo was waving his hand away when the disruptor beams struck Ruiz. He screamed in pain.

"Miranda!" Vandella cried. "Your hand!"

But she had made a snap judgment of her chances. The Romulans were on the deck they were just leaving. Going up would put distance between herself and them, but it would also leave her vulnerable, her upper body through the hatch, lower body exposed, with no way to know precisely where the enemy was.

Instead of reaching for Vandella, she released her grip on the ladder and dropped to the deck below.

Ruiz was still on his feet, blasting away at a trio of oncoming Romulans. His chest had a gaping wound, and she couldn't believe he had the strength to stand. She added her own phaser to the mix, and together they dispatched the Romulans. When the last of them had fallen, Ruiz turned toward her. His dark eyes were already glazing over. "Thanks, Miranda," he said. "Take care of . . ."

He didn't finish the sentence. His strength left him all at once, and he collapsed, falling forward into her arms. He weighed a ton, and she squatted to set him down.

And that was when the rest of the Romulans showed up, filling the far end of the corridor. Twenty of them or more, she guessed, coming her way at a fast clip.

"Miranda!" Vandella cried.

"Shoot 'em!" she shouted.

She didn't wait for him to comply. Beyond the

ladder, the corridor continued. It looked like it made a sharp turn not far ahead, so she darted that way. The Romulans were firing at her, but she weaved as she ran and their blasts missed her. Vandella and Chandler returned fire from above, holding off the Romulan advance for just long enough.

Tikolo made it to the bend and skidded into the far wall, then bounced off and continued running. She could hear the Romulan forces split up, some engaged with Vandella and Chandler, others chasing after her.

An open doorway led into an enormous space where some sort of heavy equipment had been stored. Nothing appeared connected to anything else. Storage, she thought, spare parts for the machinery used to run the ship. There were places to hide, but she couldn't see any way out except that open doorway she had entered through.

The Romulans weren't far behind. If they trapped her in here, they could hunt her down and she would have no place to go. There had to be someplace better, somewhere she could go to ground.

After a minute, she found a hatchway on her left. She wrenched the handle up. It stuck, then gave. The footfalls of the Romulans were growing louder as they neared the doorway. When they reached it, they would spot her.

The hatch was jammed shut. She tugged on it, then pushed off the wall with all her weight, and finally it swung free. She slipped through and pulled it shut behind her. It stuck in place again and she didn't worry about securing it. Chances were the Romulans wouldn't even notice it, and if they did, they would have to come through one at a time.

She was in some sort of access compartment for whatever was above her. It was pitch black, without the flat, glowing stones that illuminated the rest of the ship. The air was close and smelled heavily of lubricant, clotted and thick. She felt solid, complex structures in the dark, piping and ductwork and more. If there was another way out of the space, she would never find it.

The Romulans went past the hatchway. She willed them to keep going. At first they did; she could hear them lumbering, heavy in their battle gear. But after a few minutes they seemed to understand that she wasn't ahead of them, and they doubled back.

She was on her stomach, beneath whatever the unidentified objects were. The floor was slick with grease, and she slid farther back. Terror once again gnawed at her, the fear of the dark, of being alone. She was locked in a small space with someone dangerous outside it, and that was at once familiar and horrifying. She knew that fear had to come from somewhere, but along with most of the details of her situation, the source was lost to her.

Tikolo didn't mind, at the moment. She was

certain that if she could remember what spurred the borderline panic she felt, it would escalate into the full-blown variety. She gripped her phaser in both hands, wishing they would stop trembling. She had it pointed toward where she thought the door was, but in the dark, slipping and sliding beneath low-hanging pipes, she could no longer be entirely sure of its location.

It didn't matter that much. If anyone came in, she would see the light. Her target would be outlined against it, while she would be firing from a protected place, and closer to the ground than anyone would expect. At least the first few Romulans would die before they pinpointed her.

From the other side of the little hatch, she could hear voices, the sounds of armed soldiers. They had stopped beside the hatchway for a conference, it seemed. Tikolo wished they would move away. Her legs were starting to cramp from being wedged in, and the smell of the lubricant was getting to her. She didn't like dark, enclosed spaces, she realized, didn't like them at all. And if she didn't get out of here soon, she was going to explode.

In the distance, she heard a new voice. Another Romulan, she supposed. But the Romulans outside hushed, and it was apparent that they were listening with as much interest as she was. The voice came again, echoing down the hallways. This time, she was able to make out words. "Captain Kirk!" it called. "Mister Spock! Doctor McCoy!"

Bunker, she thought. *I don't know how I know it, but that voice belongs to Bunker.*

And Bunker was about to walk into a very bad spot.

Twenty-six

Kirk was pleasantly surprised at the bond Spock seemed to have formed with the Ixtoldan Aleshia. *Well, not really an Ixtoldan anymore,* he reasoned. A bundle of electricity without form or substance, but retaining, it seemed, at least some of what had comprised her in life. He found it hard to imagine the horror of being one of the last ones on this ship, watching those around you go mad and die. He'd had a taste of it, as a boy on Tarsus IV. The situations weren't quite the same—he had survived, after all, and so had a small handful of others. But there had been long hours when he hadn't expected that he would, when it seemed that the universe itself was coming to an end.

Since then, he had learned that death could do that. The universe—the *universes*—went on, oblivious to the lives and deaths of those within. A callous way for universes to behave, perhaps, but there it was. He liked to think that people would miss him, if the worst were to happen. People, maybe even the beings who made up Starfleet, or the Federation. Beyond that, however, the Earth would continue to spin, to carve its usual path through the Sol system. Starfleet would continue, and someone else would be made a captain and would command his ship. The Federation's efforts would go on. In the greater scheme, one individual more or less hardly mattered.

But on a more personal level, they all mattered. Everybody had someone who cared about them, someone whose day was brightened by seeing the other coming. He thought about Miranda Tikolo, who had been so isolated while the Romulans destroyed Earth Outpost 4 and all the people with whom she had served. Maybe she'd had a lover on that outpost; she was an attractive and vital woman. She had been scarred by the experience, the trauma working deep into her subconscious like a sliver under a fingernail. You couldn't just grab it and yank it; it took work to ease it out. She had been working with McCoy, trying to heal herself. The doctor had believed she was making good progress. As her captain, Kirk's concern was that she pull her weight, and remain mentally and emotionally fit for duty, and she had.

Now, if their theory was correct, her deeply buried trauma was putting everybody at risk. None of it was her fault; he had been a mess after Tarsus IV, too. If he hadn't had the calming presence of Uncle Frank and that summer on the farm, who knew what kind of disaster his life would have become? He empathized with Tikolo. He wanted to put a stop to the seemingly endless stream of Romulans attacking them, but if at all possible he wanted it done in a manner that didn't mean hurting her. If it became a question of her life weighted against the lives of the rest of the crew, then he would be the first to pull the trigger. But Kirk knew that if he did, he would always regret it, always feel that there must have been one more thing he could have tried, one more idea that might have saved her.

"Jim?" McCoy said.

"Yes, Bones?"

"How much time do you think we have left?"

"Until?"

"You heard Spock. Either we find a way off this ship or we all die."

"You're not suggesting that we leave anybody behind."

Anger flashed across McCoy's face. "Of course not! I'm just saying we'd better find those people in a hurry."

"We've been doing what we can. We'll continue to."

"Have we?"

Kirk was confused by the question. "You tell me, Bones. If there's something I haven't been doing, I'd like to know."

"Nothing against what we've tried, Jim. But now we know something we didn't before."

"What's that?"

"Spock's girlfriend. She's part of the ship's group-mind."

"Right. But where does that get us?"

"If they're all over the ship—and I think they are; I haven't felt like we've been alone for a minute—then some of them must know where the rest of our people are. If she can locate them for us . . ."

Kirk clapped McCoy on both shoulders. "Bones, you're a genius. Spock!"

Spock had been examining the remnants of what might have been a computer system. The lower decks, it turned out, had their own bunkrooms. They'd been tight, crowded quarters, with bunks stacked four high and accessed by ladders, strengthening Kirk's suspicion that there had been a rigid class system on Ixtolde, or else on Ixtolde VII—more likely the latter, since they had built the ship. Those who maintained the big engines required to move the enormous vessel through space and keep it habitable might have spent their lives down here, largely away from the denizens of the roomier, slightly more comfortable decks above.

At Kirk's call, the first officer came over. The captain filled him in on McCoy's idea. Spock's right eyebrow arched as he listened. "I can try," he said when Kirk was done. "Aleshia, are you here? Can you hear me?"

Kirk caught himself watching and listening for a response, and had to remind himself that those senses wouldn't help. But he saw a half-smile illuminate Spock's features, and he guessed that Aleshia had answered.

"We are looking for others like us," Spock said.

"In uniforms like ours. Humans, like these men and women. Their names are—"

"Bunker and Tikolo," Kirk filled in. "And Greene, Chandler, Ruiz, and Vandella. Two women, four men. If you can hear me—"

"She hears you."

"We need to find them, as quickly as we can. Before anything happens to them. You understand that, don't you?"

"She does," Spock said. "She is searching."

They stood there for long minutes. Spock's head was cocked at a slight angle, as if he were listening to a distant sound. Kirk wanted to urge Aleshia to hurry, but at the same time he had to trust Spock. The Vulcan was the only one who knew her, if that word could even be applied.

"She has located them," Spock finally said. "But they are in danger. This way, quickly." He started back the way they had just come from. Kirk hoped this didn't turn out to be a bad idea. Could Aleshia be trusted? Could Spock even be certain that this disembodied presence was the same one he had communicated with earlier? And was there a possibility, however remote, that everything Spock had told them—the whole tale of the two Ixtoldes, the invasion of the planet, the century ship that the original Ixtoldans were banished on—was a lie? Or worse, Spock's own hallucination? He could have been driven mad as easily as anyone else, couldn't he?

Now they were dashing through the hall, climbing a ladder, passing through a hatchway onto another deck. Kirk didn't remember having seen this one, though he wasn't sure how they could have skipped it. But on a ship stuck/unstuck in time and space, unhampered by the laws of physics, missing a single deck out of dozens was probably not that surprising a thing.

He was about to ask Spock for clarification, how far away they were, anything to ease his concerns, when he heard somebody calling his name. His, then Spock's, and then McCoy's. "That's Bunker," the captain said.

"Indeed it is," Spock said. "Aleshia was correct."

"He's not far away," McCoy said.

The words were barely out of his mouth when the din of combat sounded.

Tikolo felt the ship lurch. She braced herself, though she couldn't have said against what. A flash of pink light moved through the small space, like a wave surging toward shore. She watched it coming toward her, shielding her eyes against it with the flat of her hand, finally closing them when it was upon her. It warmed her as it passed, but behind it the air was cooler than before.

Instead of being where she had been—or where, given the flux of her mental state, she *believed* she had been—Tikolo was crouching at the edge of a vast plain. Two moons hung in the sky, one considerably larger than the other, and with a reddish tint. Its red glow washed the plain, upon which a bloody battle had clearly been fought.

Carnage on a scale greater than she had ever imagined was spread before her. Thousands of skulls had been piled into huge mounds. Corpses had been split open, rib cages jutting free. Carrion birds stood on or next to the carcasses, or flapped their wings for balance while dipping their heads into open cavities. More of them wheeled overhead, living black clouds of them. Fires burned here and there, sending tendrils of smoke into the sky.

She swallowed hard. The stench from the battle-field was overpowering, and her eyes watered at its assault. Was this the ultimate result of war? She had wanted to kill every Romulan she saw; her memory was fragile at the moment, but she knew that much about herself. But would her goal lead to this? Was she viewing an object lesson, or something real?

And if the latter, could she ever get back to where she had been?

Tikolo closed her eyes, trying to shut out the scene in front of her. But the stink wouldn't fade, nor would the screeching cries of all those birds. There was, she realized, something familiar about it. Not familiar in a nostalgic way, but in a terrifying one. It reminded her of something she had seen or experienced, and that had scared her so much she had blocked it from memory.

But here it was, right in front of her.

Eyes shut, she remembered a small door, a hatch, really. It had been just a short distance in front of her. There was somebody on the other side, someone shouting, and if she could just get back there, then this would all be gone and she would be safe.

She had little to lose, she thought. If she stayed at the edge of this battlefield, she would go mad. Maybe she already had. Still in a half-crouch, she moved forward, risking only quick glances through slitted eyes. She knew where she believed the hatch had been, and she pushed toward it, fighting back the almost irresistible urge to retch. She held a phaser in her right fist; with her left hand, she reached out toward where the hatch should be.

It was, she thought, the longest of shots. Tikolo pawed at the air with her left hand, and felt only the heat from the fires, the almost solid thickness of the foul night. This was a mistake, useless, and with her eyes closed, anything could be sneaking up on her. She almost opened them, then chanced another step, two.

Her hand touched something solid, metallic.

She pushed on it, eyes still clamped tight.

The hatch swung open, and she opened her eyes at last, shoving herself through. Not into a wretched field of battle, but instead into the big, mold-encrusted, filthy equipment storeroom of a starship.

"Miranda!" Bunker cried. She turned toward him.

He looked like he had just crawled off the battlefield, with cuts crisscrossing his face, and his red shirt and black pants in shreds.

She remembered him, though not like this, and then she remembered the rest of it. The dimensional fold, the shuttle trip, exploring the *McRaven* and this alien vessel. The Romulans attacking, and herself, deserting her detail. Greene and Ruiz were dead, but there were still Chandler and Vandella to worry about. "Come on, Bunker," she said. "We've got to get—"

Her sentence was cut off by the flash of a disruptor beam tearing into the wall beside them.

The Romulans were still here, waiting.

She dropped to one knee, to offer a smaller target, and fired.

Twenty-seven

Spock reached the doorway first, since only he could tell where Aleshia directed them. With the sounds of battle growing ever nearer, the captain and the rest were close behind. Suddenly he made a sharp left turn.

Ahead, the room was crowded.

Big machines lay everywhere, forgotten by time and the neglect of beings who could no longer use them.

Directly ahead were Vandella and Chandler. Beyond them was a large group of Romulans, maybe thirty strong, firing upon someone farther back. Barely shielded by some of the heavy equipment, Tikolo and Bunker were returning their fire. Vandella and Chandler appeared to have just arrived and were taking up firing positions. They would be shooting at the Romulans' backs, which didn't seem sporting except for the certainty that the Romulans would turn at the first hint of an attack from behind. Either way, the Romulans far outnumbered the *Enterprise* forces.

"Chandler, Vandella!" Kirk called. "Down!"

The two security officers glanced behind them and dropped at the same instant. The *Enterprise* landing party fired over their heads, at Romulans who were even, at that moment, whirling around and raising weapons.

The Romulans spread out through the big room, taking cover and firing in every direction. Kirk dodged a blast; the beam hit the machinery beside him and sprayed sparks across his head, scorching his face and neck. He ducked another blast and fired back. His phaser hit the shooter dead center, knocking the Romulan off his feet.

But the Romulans were scoring, too. Beachwood took a shot to the upper chest and went down hard. A disruptor beam hit Romer in the shoulder. Her phaser clattered to the deck and she fell back against one of the machines, blood gushing from the wound.

Surprise had been on their side for a moment, but that advantage was gone. The Romulans had superior numbers, and although they were caught in a cross fire, they had cover from both sides, as well.

And there would be no retreating, not with Bunker and Tikolo pinned against the far wall.

They were in for a tough, dangerous firefight, and there was no way out of it. Kirk crouched behind a hunk of machinery and took aim.

And then he saw O'Meara break from the pack and start working his way toward Tikolo. He would have to pass right by the Romulans. It was almost certain suicide. But if Kirk called out to him, that would remove the "almost." Instead, the captain kept quiet and focused on providing him cover, shooting at any Romulans who appeared to notice him.

Kirk hoped he had a plan, because from his vantage point, whatever O'Meara was doing, it was crazy.

Paul O'Meara couldn't stand the sight of Miranda, back against the wall, facing dozens of Romulans with only a beat-up Bunker beside her. Captain Kirk and the others would help, but even with that additional force, the Romulans had the numerical advantage, and it would only take one shot to kill the woman he loved. For the last several hours he had been roaming this crazy ship, desperate to find her, wondering where she was, wondering if he would ever see her again.

He saw what looked like an opening and he went for it. There was an area along the near wall to which the Romulans paid scant attention, because none of their opponents were there. If he could move quickly and quietly, maybe he could reach Miranda. Then, if the theory Mister Spock had put forth was correct, he could talk to her, make her understand that the Romulans had been brought here by her own troubled mind.

If the theory was wrong, at least they could die together.

O'Meara walked in a hunched-over position, trying to combine speed with safety. Glancing back once, he caught Kirk's gaze and realized the captain was tracking his progress, firing at Romulans who spotted him. To fire himself would give away his position and his plan.

Finally, he reached the end of his cover. Before him was a stretch of two meters, almost three, where there were none of the pieces of machinery he had used to shield his progress so far. He would have to cross the open space before he could reach cover behind the equipment shielding Miranda and Bunker.

He looked toward the Romulans. They were engaged with the *Enterprise* landing party. Close combat required focus, and they were giving it their all. He might have been able to tap one of them on the shoulder without being seen until he did.

He wouldn't get a better chance. O'Meara broke from cover and sprinted toward Miranda. No shots came his way. He made it to the first piece of machinery and called her name. "Miranda!" She turned her head and looked his way, and when he saw those eyes meeting his, he thought that he might break down and weep. "Miranda," he said again, slowing to a crouching walk. "I'm so glad—"

• • •

Tikolo wasn't ready to die—she didn't know if any-body ever was—but she thought her time had come. She and Bunker were backed against a wall, facing down thirty or so Romulans looking for a fight. Van-della and Chandler came in after the Romulans, but that was still only four against a horde.

She and Bunker took refuge behind some pieces of unknown machinery, big enough to block their disruptors. For a while, at least. They fired at the Romulans, the Romulans fired back, and battle was joined.

Then, salvation, or at least its promise, appeared in the form of Captain Kirk and the rest of the landing party. She noticed that a few were missing, but they still helped to make the odds less lopsided.

Everything that had happened had worn her down. Her mental lapses had made things worse, and although she believed she was better, she still had a hard time trusting her own judgment. Being fired on by Romulans, intent on killing her as they had her crewmates on Outpost 4, rocked her self-confidence to its core.

Then one of them broke from the pack and charged toward her from the side. His mouth was open, he was saying something, and it sounded almost like her name, but it couldn't be that, how could a Romulan know that? She raised her phaser and saw fear enter his eyes and she squeezed the trigger and fired, and her beam caught him full in the chest. He threw his arms out to his sides, hands going loose, and his weapon (and was that a phaser, not a disruptor?— maybe he had picked it up from the body of a slain crew member) flew away. She fired once more, though he was already falling.

Kirk watched in horror as Tikolo fired at O'Meara, then fired again. He had been close enough that she must have seen him, couldn't have failed to recognize that familiar face.

Unless, Kirk realized, she in fact could not recognize him because Tikolo herself was only partly there. The mental stress of these past hours must have been terrible; he didn't know where she had been or what she had gone through, but it hadn't been a stroll through the bowels of the ship.

She might have thought they were all Romulans, might fire at him or Spock or Chandler next. He adjusted his phaser, setting it to stun—not sure if it would work—and darted to where O'Meara had begun his cautious trek to Tikolo. Except O'Meara had had Kirk to provide him cover fire. Still, the battle was fierce; no one was paying attention to him, on either side.

He started toward Tikolo and Bunker, employing the same shelter O'Meara had used. He tried to move faster than O'Meara had, knowing that all it would take was for one Romulan to spot him. He would be an easy target, especially when he had to cross that open ground.

The captain kept hoping he'd have a shot at Tikolo, but she was using cover well, coming out only long enough to snap off a blast at whatever Romulan she had in her sights. From this angle, he could see only bits of her arm, sometimes a shoulder or a brief glimpse of that lustrous black hair.

He would have to do what O'Meara had done—dash across the open space—and take his shot when he got there. That meant he would have to be faster than she was. She was younger, scared, battling for her life, and possibly completely delusional.

Kirk didn't like his chances.

He broke into the open.

The captain had barely taken a step when a Romulan he hadn't noticed before rose from cover, homing in on him with a disruptor, leading him just a little. If he turned to fire, it would put him off balance, slow his dash toward Tikolo. And his phaser was only set on stun. He had to keep his momentum, hurtle forward, hope the warrior missed.

Kirk was turning his head away, watching Bunker and Tikolo, knowing that once he had a clear shot he had to take it fast, when he saw the Romulan lifted bodily off the deck—by what, Kirk couldn't tell—and hurled into his comrades.

Aleshia! he thought. And then he was face-to-face with Tikolo. Her phaser was coming up to fire.

Kirk shot first.

The beam hit her and she froze, then fell backward. Her weapon slipped from numbed fingers. Bunker spun toward Kirk, then lowered his phaser, a smile spreading across his face.

"I knew you'd come, Captain," he said. "The whole time I was out there, lost, I knew you'd be looking for me."

"We were," Kirk said. "Tikolo was. Why did you run off?"

"I thought I saw my sister," Bunker said. "She was scared and running for her life. Only she's been dead for eleven years now. So I flipped out, I guess. I'm sorry."

"It's that kind of place," Kirk said.

"But all we gotta do now is make it out alive, right? Through all of them."

Kirk looked. "All of who?" he asked.

The Romulans were gone. They had come from Tikolo's mind, and now that it was shut down—for the moment, at least—so were they.

But Kirk had to get them off this ship before she came to. Or deal with whatever her troubled psyche might materialize next.

He thought the former option was preferable to the latter. "Let's go, people," he said. "Let's get the bodies of those who didn't make it, and get out of here."

He had barely spoken when the ship shook. No

quick lurch this time; the entire vessel seemed to vibrate for thirty seconds or more. When it ended, nothing had visibly changed.

"That felt like—" McCoy began.

"Captain," Spock interrupted. "I believe we're being fired upon."

Twenty-eight

"Mister Scott!" Chekov said. Scotty had just stepped onto the bridge.

"Aye?"

"The *Ton'bey* just fired at that large wessel. The one in the middle of the dimensional fold."

"The one we think the away team is on?" Scott asked.

"The same."

"Did they hit it?"

"I cannot be sure," Chekov said. "It appeared that the fold might have deflected it to some extent, but I believe they did."

"I believe this calls for a swift and certain response," the engineeer said. He stormed back toward the captain's chair.

"Is that an order?" Chekov asked. Hope was written across his face.

Scotty scowled, considering the options. He wanted to give the order. But he couldn't simply give in to his immediate urge; he had to try to do what was best for the Federation.

"Uhura, hail the *Ton'bey*. Order them to stand

down. Tell 'em that under no circumstances are they to discharge their weapons again. If they do, they'll suffer the most severe consequences."

"Aye, sir," Uhura said. She spun around to her station and started hailing the Ixtoldan ship.

"What's next?" Chekov asked.

"Next I'm gonna have a serious talk with that Chan'ya creature. And if I don't like what she has to say . . ."

"Yes?"

"Well, you might still have a chance to launch her from a torpedo tube."

"I am," Chekov said, "eternally optimistic."

"Who would shoot at us?" Kirk asked.

"Maybe the Romulan ship, sir?" Chandler suggested.

"There *are* no Romulan ships. The Romulans we fought were manifested by Tikolo's subconscious mind." The captain waved his hand around the now Romulan-free space. "As you can see, when she lost consciousness, they vanished."

"If I may, Captain," Spock said. "The most logical suspect is the Ixtoldan battle cruiser, the *Ton'bey*."

"Explain."

"Although no Ixtoldan histories I encountered in my prior research mentioned this vessel, we know it originated on Ixtolde, and we know its background. The usurpers of Ixtolde rewrote the histories of that planet to suit their own ends. But these events happened in the relatively recent past, and there have been, no doubt, stories handed down through the generations. I believe that as we approached the dimensional fold, the Ixtoldans, both on the *Enterprise* and the *Ton'bey,* recognized this ship. They did not want us anywhere near it."

"Which is why Minister Chan'ya was so adamant that we continue on to Ixtolde, instead of stopping to investigate," Kirk provided.

"Indeed. She tried everything within her power to encourage us to bypass the fold. When you announced that you would board the *McRaven,* to learn what had happened to her crew, she tried to set time limits on the away mission. By this point, we have been here long enough that the minister suspects her worst fears have been realized. She believes that we have learned the truth about this ship, and therefore about the takeover of Ixtolde. She knows that such a revelation would eliminate any chance of Ixtolde being admitted into the Federation. Ixtolde is the last planet in their system that has even a fighting chance of survival, but true survival depends upon the trade advantages that Federation membership brings. Therefore, she is determined to destroy the evidence—and us with it."

"But, surely she knows that firing on this ship, with the *Enterprise* right there, would bring about the same result. There's no way the *Enterprise* wouldn't report the *Ton'bey's* actions."

"Presumably she does, Captain. Which simply means

that once the *Ton'bey* has destroyed this ship, its captain will have little choice but to also destroy the *Enterprise*. For that matter, we have been here for several hours, at least. We cannot know if the *Ton'bey* has been joined by other Ixtoldan warships, or if the *Enterprise* has already been bested."

Spock's words sent an uncomfortable tingle down Kirk's spine. He was right, of course. They'd had no communication with the *Enterprise* since before they had set foot on the Ixtoldan vessel. Although he believed in his crew, the fact remained that they were relatively close to Ixtoldan space. If reinforcements from Ixtolde had arrived, the *Enterprise* might have been surrounded and outgunned.

"The Ixtoldans—the current ones, those who have assumed the planetary identity—have made a series of bad decisions," Spock went on. "They invaded a neighboring planet rather than attempting to work out another solution to their dilemma. They eliminated all traces of the previous population, or so they thought. Believing that to be the case, they applied for Federation membership. When we set a course for their stolen planet, we did not know it would take us so near the dimensional fold, nor did we know that the *McRaven* would stumble into it. But having done so, they were at a moment of crisis. They had to hope we would not venture into the fold, and when we did, they had to try to prevent us from emerging with the evidence of their deeds. From the first shelling of the original Ixtoldans, they have had to take every step possible to cover up their crimes, and each step has led only to another lie, another cover-up."

"'Oh what a tangled web we weave,'" McCoy quoted.

"We need to get off this ship," Kirk said. "And back to the *Enterprise*." The captain started toward the door of the big room. They still had crew members to recover. They'd lost too many already; he had to know if the *Enterprise* was safe.

They retraced the steps of the search party first, finding the bodies of Ruiz and Greene. Then they headed back to the upper decks, where they had lost others. En route, Spock stepped closer to Kirk, and spoke in low tones. "Captain," he said. "I appreciate the urgency of leaving this ship behind, but if I may offer a suggestion?"

"By all means."

"This vessel has been trapped here far too long, and the Ixtoldans on board, not living but also not quite dead, have been trapped here as well, due to the peculiar nature of the fold."

"Are you proposing we try to get it out?"

"I am proposing that the ship should not be left here. Not just for the sake of the Ixtoldans here, but to prevent other ships, like the *McRaven,* from interacting with it. This ship is a death trap. We are fortunate that more of us have not succumbed."

"We're not off it yet," Kirk pointed out.

"True," Spock said.

"Do you have any ideas as to how we might do this?"

"I do not, but I will give the matter all consideration."

"Until then, we have to get back to the *Enterprise*," Kirk said.

The landing party had recovered all of their dead and carried them back to the juncture between the Ixtoldan ship and the *McRaven*. The environmental suits were still there, but some could be left behind. Kirk hoped a single shuttle could take the weight of the entire landing party, since getting out of the fold might be too complicated to do more than once.

Gathering up their environmental suits, the *Enterprise* landing party worked their way through the *McRaven*. Kirk thought about Spock's request to free the Ixtoldan ship from the dimensional fold. They would need power, and lots of it, to break it out of the fold's grip. The ship had been stuck for a long time, and the chaotic nature of the fold had added years, centuries. The chances of getting its engines powered up were slim.

But there was still the *McRaven*. It had been in the fold for only a matter of days, as measured from outside the fold. Chances were, despite whatever bouncing around through dimensions and universes the *McRaven* had done, its power systems were still intact. If they could be brought back on line, maybe the *McRaven* could pull the Ixtoldan ship free.

"Change of plans," Kirk said at the junction that led to the hangar deck. "We're going to the bridge."

"Not the hangar deck, Captain?" Vandella asked.

"It's time to take the offensive."

"I hope you know what you're doing, Jim," McCoy whispered in the captain's ear.

"Bones, have you heard of flying by the seat of your pants?"

"Of course I have."

"Well, that's what we're going to do. Seat of the pants all the way."

McCoy looked sour. "I got a feeling I'm gonna wish my pants were armor-plated," he said.

"Oh, you are. You definitely are."

Twenty-nine

Remarkably, the *McRaven*'s impulse engines powered up.

They were a long way from out of the woods. There was no indication that the ship would be able to escape the fold's grip on its own, much less towing the huge Ixtoldan vessel. If they could have escaped, Kirk was sure its crew would have done so, rather than be drawn deeper into the fold.

But he wasn't counting on its being able to get free on its own. He wanted its power for other purposes.

"It's not full power, Captain," Bunker said. "We couldn't reach full impulse, and the warp drive is inoperable. But you have power, sir."

"Thank you, Mister Bunker," Kirk said. He went to the communications station and hailed the *Enterprise*. After a moment, he heard Uhura's voice, faint but unmistakable.

"*Cap . . . that you? We've . . . about . . .*"

"It's me, Uhura," Kirk said. "Your signal is weak, but I can read you faintly. Do you read me?"

"*Boosting sig . . . tain,*" came back.

"Can you do anything here to boost our signal,

Bunker? We've got to cut through whatever interference the fold is creating."

"I'll try, sir," Bunker said. He dropped to the deck and removed one of the service bay panels at deck level, then scooted his upper torso inside.

The ship shook violently again. Kirk had felt earthquakes, and the rumble and shudder reminded him of that. "The Ixtoldan ship just took another plasma burst, Captain," Spock reported. "We are feeling the effects because the *McRaven* is still joined to the Ixtoldan vessel."

"Can you read me, Uhura? Is the *Ton'bey* firing into the dimensional fold?"

"*Yes, Captain.*" Uhura's voice was stronger now— the efforts on their side, or Bunker's work, or both, had helped. "*Mister Scott is formulating the appropriate response. After they fired the first time, we told them that any further offensive action would be considered an act of war.*"

"Tell Mister Scott to hold off," Kirk said. "I think we need them."

"*But Captain, they're firing on—*"

"On an empty ship," Kirk said. "Or essentially empty. At any rate, we need the *Ton'bey* whole for now. Someone will have to approach Minister Chan'ya."

"*Mister Scott read her the riot act,*" Uhura said. "*She might not be in a cooperative mood.*"

"Let her know that this is her only chance. Ixtolde won't be admitted into the Federation any time soon—probably not in her lifetime. But she has a chance to avoid sanctions being leveled against her people for genocide. And when Ixtolde is deemed ready to apply again, many, many years from now, her cooperation at this time will be remembered. She has nothing left to lose and everything to gain by cooperating."

"*We'll make that clear, sir. What is your plan?*"

The captain described what he had in mind.

When he had broken the connection, McCoy gave him a grin. "That's downright clever, Jim," he said. "How'd you come up with that?"

Kirk settled himself into the *McRaven*'s captain's chair. The entire landing party was on the bridge, using every available seat and sprawled out on the floor. The fallen were already stowed in the shuttle, but Tikolo was here, still unconscious. With the unreliability of the phaser within the fold, he had hit her a with a deeper stun than expected, or else her system was just so damaged that it had affected her harder than usual. They were still within the fold, though not on the Ixtoldan ship, so the captain was not sorry she was still out. Kirk looked around, knowing that every face would be turned his way. "Uncle Frank."

"Uncle Frank?" McCoy echoed.

"He was a farmer," Kirk said. "He grew corn, winter wheat, sorghum, whatever there was a need for. But Idaho was also ranching country, and he had friends in the ranching community."

"What's the difference?" Chandler asked.

"In the most simplistic terms," Spock said, "a farmer raises crops and a rancher raises livestock."

"Winter comes early in Idaho," Kirk explained. "And traditional ranchers still drive their cattle to winter pastures in the late summer. In that rugged country, cows don't stick close to the roads, and aerial drives are impractical. To move the herds, you've got to be on the ground, where they are. That means on horseback."

"You were a cowboy, sir?" Vandella asked.

"For a couple of weeks, yes," Kirk said with a smile. "I was a cowboy."

McCoy laughed. "Jimmy Kirk in a big hat on an even bigger horse."

"I was a pretty good-sized kid," Kirk said. "Skinny, but tall. I'll grant you, it was probably a comical sight," he admitted. "But I did what I could to help out." He remembered horseback climbs up and down treacherous slopes, where a misplaced hoof could have spelled injury or death for the inexperienced rider. Uncle Frank had put a lot of faith in him, and he had returned that faith tenfold, trusting that his uncle would keep him safe no matter what. "Anyway, we were on that cattle drive for days and days, and hungry cowboys have got to eat."

"A chuck wagon?" McCoy asked. The doctor had traveled to distant stars, but the idea of an old-fashioned chuck wagon seemed to fill him with wonder.

"A chuck wagon, pulled by a single mule. But on one occasion, on a steep uphill grade, that mule couldn't do the job by itself." In his mind's eye, Kirk saw the chuck wagon again, all old, rough wood and heavy iron fittings, and that brown mule with the big ears and the teeth that had seemed gigantic to him. It had tried and tried to get that wagon up the hill, until finally the cook had to jump down off his bench and tell it to quit before it had a heart attack. The mule had sat down, glaring back over its shoulder at the wagon and braying.

"In a sense," he continued, "that job was like this one. Everybody knew their job. If a wagon wheel broke, someone could fix it. If a calf was trapped in a thorny thicket, someone could coax it out and someone else could dress its wounds. They went where they had to go and did what they had to do to get the job done. At night, around the campfire, there was complaining and grousing and stories and songs. It was beautiful."

"So, like this," Bunker said. "But without the need for astrophysics or advanced quantum mechanics."

"Right. The experienced hands decided to hitch a second animal to the wagon. They picked my horse, a big stallion named Champ. What one mule couldn't do on its own, the mule and Champ accomplished. They put their backs and legs and hearts into it, and they got that wagon up the hill."

"Which is where the old term 'horsepower' comes from," McCoy offered. "Champ added just enough horsepower to get the job done."

"Your plan makes perfect sense now, Captain," Bunker said.

Before Kirk could respond, the comm crackled and Uhura's voice sounded. "*We're in place and ready to go, Captain,*" she said.

"Let's get it started, Uhura. We'll do what we can on this end."

"*Aye, aye, sir.*"

"Places, everyone," Kirk said. He kept his seat at the captain's chair, and Spock took his usual place at the science station. Bunker took the helm and Romer, her shoulder wrapped in a bandage, sat at the navigation station.

"We're ready, Uhura," Kirk said.

"Easy, now," Scotty warned. "Not too sudden. We dinna want to tear the *McRaven* apart."

"Aye, sir," Chekov said. "I must point out, we don't know how hard the *Ton'bey* is pulling."

Scotty wished he were handling the tractor beam controls. If it became necessary he could relieve Chekov and take over. He didn't doubt the ensign's abilities, but he was an engineer at heart and he preferred to do it himself. Delegating did not come easily to him.

"Just ease it out of there," Scotty said. "The captain

said they don't have much power, but he'll add thrust when he can."

The engineer watched the viewscreen, which the *McRaven*'s image had been magnified to fill. "The trouble is, she's attached to that big ship," Chekov said.

"Aye, lad," Scotty said. "We all understand Sir Isaac's first law."

"I'm trying to maintain a lock on the *McRaven*, but there's so much extra mass."

"Steady," Scott ordered. *That's why the* Ton'bey *is also pulling,* Scotty thought. Captain Kirk had told them where to position the two ships, and at what angle to pull from. The captain had said something about horsepower, but Scott attributed that to the poor communication link—the pull of a starship's tractor beam was far too powerful to be measured by such primitive standards. The idea was to wrench the *McRaven* and the Ixtoldan ship away from those clustered around them.

It was all made more complicated by the uncertain nature of the dimensional fold. The reverse tractor beam had worked initially, pushing the shuttles into the fold; therefore, it should work to draw the ships out. But from Scotty's limited understanding of the fold, the pair of tractor beams might be converted, once inside the boundaries of the fold, to something entirely unhelpful.

"We have movement," Sulu declared suddenly.

Scott had taken his eyes off the screen for a

moment. He looked again and saw that Sulu was right. The *McRaven* was shuddering—not, his experienced eyes told him, breaking apart—and so was the Ixtoldan ship joined to it. Some of the other vessels around them were also being pulled out, but that was to be expected.

"Easy," he said. "Easy does it, lad."

"Aye, sir." Chekov said, his hands shaking with the strain of controlling the beam.

Scotty slumped back in the captain's chair. This *had* to work.

He wouldn't allow himself to conceive of any other possibility.

Thirty

The noise was awful.

The *McRaven* was joined to the Ixtoldan starship, and other ships were connected to that one as well, as if they'd been welded into one gigantic sculpture. As Bunker goosed the thrusters, applying brief bursts that they hoped would help the dual tractor beams pull the *McRaven* and its Ixtoldan counterpart free from the mass, the sound of groaning, straining metal reverberated all through the ship. Kirk felt it in his bones.

Come on, girl, hold together.

The captain allowed himself a fleeting grin. The noise meant something was happening. The tractor beams were having an effect.

He checked the bridge's main viewscreen. The nose-in configuration in which the *McRaven* had joined with the Ixtoldan ship meant that the screen was mostly filled with the other vessel's battered exterior. Its surface looked like something that might have dated from Earth's Industrial Ages, pitted and rusted, scraped and scarred. At the upper edge of the screen, some of the other ships were partially visible.

As the horrendous racket continued, Kirk could see movement. The Ixtoldan ship shifted noticeably, causing a ripple effect. "More thrust," he ordered.

"Yes, sir," Bunker said, adjusting the controls.

The Ixtoldan ship shifted, moving toward the *McRaven*. It completely filled the viewscreen, to the point that his crew members were leaning back from their stations. At the last instant, it stopped with a deafening squeal. At the top of the screen, Kirk noted, one of the previously attached ships had been jarred loose from the rest and was beginning to drift away.

"We're making progress," he said. "More thrust." Activating the comm, Kirk said, "*Enterprise*. Mister Scott, can you increase the tractor beam output?"

"*We're givin' you everything we got, Captain,*" Scotty answered. "*But I'll see if I can find you a wee bit more.*"

"Understood, *Enterprise*. *McRaven* out."

"Mister Bunker, can you get any more out of the *McRaven*'s thrusters?"

"I'm trying, sir, but it's a delicate balance. We're liable to tear the ship apart."

"Give it a good burst and then shut them down," Kirk said. "See if we can't rock her free."

The ships gave another mighty groan, and the Ixtoldan craft loomed closer. When it heaved back, the ancient Romulan bird-of-prey had torn loose.

"What was that?" McCoy asked.

"The pull of the tractor beams, I believe," Spock answered. "We are only marginally in control of this effort. The Ixtoldan vessel, caught between us and the mass of other starships, has its own momentum now and is rocking back and forth."

"We need to try to rip the Ixtoldan ship away from those other vessels without letting it smash too hard against us," Kirk said. "If it destroys the *McRaven*, we're trapped here."

"We're counting on whatever the force joined the *McRaven* to it a few days ago being stronger than whatever seals exist between that monster and other ships that might have held for hundreds of years?"

"That about sums it up, Bones, yes."

McCoy shook his head. "The things I let you talk me into."

"Mister Bunker, sharp acceleration now, then shut down," Kirk ordered.

Bunker complied. The *McRaven* pulled with the Ixtoldan ship's roll. The thrust was accompanied by another terrible screech of metal against metal. Then the Ixtoldan ship completely filled the viewscreen and made contact with the *McRaven*'s upper saucer section. The sound of impact was the loudest yet, a crash like all the thunder Kirk had ever known roaring at once. The force knocked people from chairs, threw others to the deck. Sparks flew from instrumentation around the bridge.

"Status report!" Kirk commanded.

"There is some instrument damage," Spock said after a brief diagnostic check. "But the systems in use appear to be operational."

"Thrusters are still on line," Bunker reported.

"We've moved, Captain," Romer said. "Not a significant amount, but measurable, and in the right direction. Toward the *Enterprise*."

Uhura's voice sounded over the comm system again. "McRaven, *are you all right over there?*"

"We're fine," Kirk replied.

"*I don't know if you can see it from there, but you and the Ixtoldan ship have separated from most of the vessels around it. There are still a handful hanging on, but that's all.*"

"That's good to know," Kirk said. "Keep those tractor beams pulling."

"*Roger.* Enterprise *out,*" Uhura said.

"We're getting somewhere," Kirk said. "We can't let up now."

"Sir," Bunker said, "the *McRaven* might not hold up to another hit like that."

"That's a risk we'll have to take," Kirk replied. "Give us another quick thrust. Let's try to jar the rest of those ships loose."

Bunker swallowed and obeyed his captain's orders. The *McRaven* tugged and the Ixtoldan vessel followed, faster without the weight of the others holding it back. And again it made impact, although without as much force behind it. The starship shook and complained, but held together.

"Keep it up," Kirk said. "Keep rocking her. Once we've shed enough weight, those tractor beams will do the rest."

"Aye, sir," Romer said. "The sooner we're out of this anomaly, the better I'll like it."

"That," Spock replied, "may fairly be said of us all."

Miranda Tikolo's head was pounding, and she kept hearing sounds like the fiery breath of dragons. After a while, she realized that she had been asleep, and that wakefulness was just on the other side of a thin but resistant veil. She struggled toward it, writhing and moaning with the effort.

"Easy, Miranda," a gentle voice said, close to her ear. "Take it easy. You're safe now."

"Is she waking up, Doctor?" another voice said. Both voices were familiar, though she couldn't place them.

"Looks that way." She felt a firm pressure on her shoulder. "You're all right."

"Miranda," the second voice said. "Miranda, can you hear me?"

Tikolo tried to answer, but all she heard issue from her mouth was a squeak. She tore at the veil. Another roar sounded and the floor beneath her shuddered. "Whuh?" she managed.

"Don't pay that any attention," the first voice said. "That doesn't concern you, Miranda."

"She's coming around, isn't she?"

"Yes, Stanley. She's coming around. But don't push her. Let it happen at her own speed."

Stanley. She *knew* that name. His was the second voice, and the first one belonged to . . .

She blinked, and a lined, friendly face hovered before her. Doctor McCoy; *his* was the first voice. She opened her eyes again, held them that way for several seconds before her eyelids fluttered closed again.

Someone—Stanley, she thought—gripped her right hand. Doctor McCoy was on her left. She was on her back, lying on something hard. And her head would not quit throbbing. Her stomach churned, and she tasted bile.

"You're going to be just fine, Miranda," McCoy said.

She forced her eyes open once more. McCoy was crouched on the floor beside her. Turning her head made the throbbing worse and her nausea flare, but she saw Stanley sitting on her right, cross-legged on the floor, clutching her hand in both of his. His face was creased with worry.

"Miranda!" he said, his voice thick with emotion. "How do you feel? Are you okay?"

"Th . . . the doctor says . . . I am," Tikolo replied. It took all the effort she could muster to force those words out.

"You were stunned, that's all," McCoy said. "It's a

shock to the system, but there won't be any permanent effects."

"That's . . . good," she said weakly. "Because head . . . hurts like a son-of-a-bitch."

Vandella barked a sudden laugh. "That's my gloriously blunt Miranda," he said, crushing her hand in his.

"You're perfectly safe now, Miranda. How much do you remember?" McCoy asked her.

Panic shot through her. She tried to fight it back. Vandella and McCoy were right beside her, flanking her. There had been Romulans, but they appeared to be gone. She shifted her head, trying to ignore the queasiness, and took in a *Constitution*-class bridge. Somehow she knew it was not the *Enterprise.*

"That other ship," she said. "Romulans . . . attacking us. Are they . . . ?"

"All gone, Miranda," McCoy said. "Nothing to worry about now."

Memories flooded back to her then. The fight against the Romulans, when she and Bunker were pinned against a wall and facing overwhelming odds. Before that, she had been someplace close, tight, and looking at a vast battlefield. Tikolo remembered, although she had not at the time, that the battlefield was one from nightmares she'd had as a child and a teen, a recurring dream that had never failed to leave her gasping for breath, twisted in sheets she had soaked with sweat. She had forgotten the dream, couldn't even remember the last time she'd had it, but she suspected it was before she entered Starfleet Academy. This time she had not been asleep, she was certain of that, but her mental state had been confused. There were gaps in her memory, places she couldn't recall what had happened, and her time on the Ixtoldan ship was a series of flashes, like life viewed under a strobe light.

"Can I . . . sit up?" she asked.

"I'd rather you didn't yet," McCoy said. He pressed a hypo against her neck. "But if you take it real easy, then okay."

The doctor and Vandella helped her to her elbows, but that was as far as she could go. Even with the hypo she felt dizzy; the bridge swam before her in sickening waves.

She saw familiar faces: the captain, Mister Spock, Eve Chandler, and others. There were some she didn't see, however: Greene, Ruiz, Beachwood, O'Meara.

"Paul?" she said. "Where's Paul?"

"I'm afraid he didn't make it," McCoy replied. "We'll talk about that later. The important thing is that you're safe. You're—"

A terrible grinding noise drowned out whatever the doctor said next, and the floor jerked beneath her. She lost her balance and her head dropped toward the floor, but McCoy's hand was there first, catching her and easing her down gently. She smiled up toward his kindly face.

"We have a lot to talk about, Miranda," he said. "First we have to get back to the *Enterprise,* and when we do that, we'll have a nice long chat."

"That . . . sounds good," she said. Her eyelids fluttered again, and she let them close.

Thirty-one

The viewscreen told the story. Their last thrust had succeeded in breaking the *McRaven* free from the Ixtoldan vessel, and that one from the rest of the pack.

"Steady on the thrusters, Mister Bunker," Kirk said. "*Enterprise*, keep those tractor beams locked on us and the other ship."

"*You're making good progress, Captain,*" Uhura replied. "*Just a few more minutes and you will clear the anomaly.*"

Kirk hoped she was right. The dimensional fold had not played any of its tricks for a while, but he remembered how unsettling it had been on the way in.

He had other concerns, as well. "Environmental suits on. We don't know how much damage was done to the hull when the ships separated, but it's entirely possible that our atmospheric system will fail at any moment. We'll stay suited up until we're safely on board the *Enterprise*."

What was left of the landing party complied with his instructions. McCoy and Vandella put on their own suits, then helped Tikolo into hers.

Kirk had just taken the center seat again when the viewscreen went blank.

"What was that?" McCoy asked.

"The screen is fully functional," Spock said.

Kirk stared at it. It was not quite white, not black, not exactly gray. He couldn't pin a color to it. As he held his gaze on it, it came to him that this might have been what the end of the universe looked like. No, not that—*beyond* the end of the universe. The universe was full of stars and dark matter, pulsars and cosmic rays, red giants and white dwarfs and black holes and unexplained anomalies. But this—the view outside the *McRaven,* if the screen could be believed—was nothingness. Empty. Simply . . . absence.

Looking at it chilled Kirk to his core. He tore his gaze away and saw that it had the same effect on the others. They watched with eyes wide, mouths agape, and more than a few were trembling at the sight.

Although it lasted less than a minute, it was a sight he would remember for the rest of his life. Reality, Kirk was learning, was surpassingly strange stuff. The physics he had studied only scratched at the surface of what was out here. The *Enterprise* was on a five-year mission of exploration, but that mission could be extended to five lifetimes, five millennia, and still there would be more to discover.

Without warning, the nothingness beyond the universe's edge was replaced with a view back toward the Ixtoldan ship, only the ship was corkscrewing on itself, and flares of bright pink light were shooting past it faster than the eye could follow. Then that image reversed—not into a mirror image, but an actual reversal, as if the *McRaven* had skipped to the other side of the Ixtoldan ship in the blink of an eye. The pink flares were going in the opposite direction, and the ship itself was coming out of its impossible twist. Finally, the screen went briefly black, then returned to its normal view. The Ixtoldan ship had drifted a little farther away, but both vessels continued on the same course.

The *McRaven* lurched once, and what felt like a wave of energy passed through those on board.

Uhura's voice came over the comm, loud and clear. "McRaven. *You're out!*"

"What about the other vessel?" Spock asked.

"*Give it a few seconds,*" Uhura said. "*. . . Also clear.*"

Spock left his seat at the science station and crossed to the viewscreen, as if it might show him what was happening on board the Ixtoldan century ship.

Kirk joined him there. "Spock?" he asked. The other ship was floating away from theirs, more distant with every second that passed.

"I sense the liberation of all those prisoners."

"Prisoners?"

"They were sentenced to that ship. They did not ask to be, and many fought back, but the invaders were too strong, too technologically advanced, to be resisted. When they boarded that ship, the Ixtoldans believed that they would drift through space for a time, to live and procreate, and that someday they would find a new homeworld. Instead, they became trapped in the dimensional fold. No one could survive that for long, and they did not.

"Their fate, however, was not precisely death. Now they will die—are, perhaps, already dying as we watch. But they are doing so while soaring through space. This is, no doubt, a vastly preferable end. Aleshia told me that she looked forward to it, and so did the others."

"And the ship itself," Kirk added. "A living ship, thanks to its group-mind, and a ghost ship at the same time. Now it too can rest."

"Indeed," Spock said. "It is more than ready." His right hand rose to his chest, just for an instant, and then he dropped it and turned away. Kirk figured that it was a salute, however unconscious. He brought his own hand to his chest, and held it there as he watched the Ixtoldans drift toward eternity.

"Torpedoes are ready, Captain," Sulu reported.

"Thank you, Mister Sulu," Kirk said. He was back in *his* chair on the *Enterprise* bridge, a seat he found considerably more comfortable than its counterpart on the *McRaven*.

"Locked on target."

"Fire torpedo one."

"Firing torpedo one."

In a matter of seconds, Kirk saw the photon torpedo streaking through space toward the *McRaven*. After the landing party, including the fallen, had been beamed back aboard, Kirk had ordered the *Enterprise* moved a safe distance away. The *McRaven* was beyond salvage.

"Fire torpedo two," Kirk ordered.

"Firing torpedo two."

A second photon torpedo shot out from beneath the *Enterprise*'s saucer section. The first struck the *McRaven*'s secondary hull and a massive explosion bloomed. Instants later, the second torpedo joined it. The two blasts merged into one brilliant, breathtaking event, reminding Kirk that there could be beauty in destruction. Spock had earlier drawn his attention to the possibility of nobility in death.

Devastating wars on Earth had led, eventually, to peace, hope, and with first contact, the uniting of the planet in a spirit of optimism. That spirit had created Starfleet, which sent ships out to explore the limitless depths of space. Watching as a ball of fierce, hot energy engulfed the *McRaven*, Kirk was reminded that death was as much a part of life as birth and everything in between. Fragments of the ship spewed in every direction, and they would float forever in space, but within seconds the bulk of the ship had been vaporized, and the visual aspect of the explosion was sucked back into itself and then vanished.

"I hate to see any Starfleet vessel end up like that," Sulu said. "Especially at my hands."

Kirk got up and placed a hand on the helmsman's shoulder. "It was good that she had you to speed her along."

Sulu offered a grateful smile. Straightening his dress uniform, the captain said, "Duty calls. I've got to get down to the transporter room, to see our guests off."

Minister Chan'ya tried to present a proud aspect, but Kirk could tell she was under incredible stress. He recognized that the lines around her eyes and the corners of her mouth had grown deeper over the past few days. Her skin was paler than he had ever seen it, and she stood with her shoulders slightly hunched, as though she had given up all hope of ever being as tall as some in her retinue.

"You'll be beamed to the *Ton'bey* now," Kirk told her. They were already in place on the transporter platform, waiting for the captain's arrival. "I know you understand that Ixtolde's application for Federation membership will be denied. We had hoped that Ixtolde was ready to join; plainly that was not the case."

"We regret our actions," Chan'ya said. "And our deceptions, however slight. We were in a precarious ethical position, and we should have made better choices. Your hospitality, Captain Kirk, is appreciated."

One of her companions grunted at that, and made

a sour face. Kirk didn't think it was worth commenting on.

"Do you know what's in store for you?" Kirk asked. "When you get home?"

"Some form of punishment, we imagine," Chan'ya said. "What form it will take, we know not. Shame, at best. Perhaps banishment. Perhaps something more severe."

"But you were only playing the cards others dealt," Kirk said. "That might be an Earth-centric reference, but—"

"We understand the metaphor, Captain. It is true that we did not make the original decisions that led us to this point. Generations before us did, and what has occurred cannot be changed. Nonetheless, the punishment will be what it is determined to be, and it will come down hardest upon us. And the command staff of the *Ton'bey*."

"Have you considered not going home? If the captain and crew are in for discipline, too, over something that was really beyond their control . . ."

Chan'ya caught the eye of someone else in her party, the one he thought was Keneseth. Her skin turned a little more golden, and something that might have been a smile passed between them. "Never," she said. "The duty of Ixtoldans is to Ixtolde."

"Of course," Kirk said. "Just thought I'd mention it."

"Well and good. We thank you, Captain. And now, we must take our leave."

Kirk nodded to the transporter tech, who worked the controls. The Ixtoldans glimmered, glittered, and were gone.

Happy to be back on his own ship, secure in more or less predictable reality, Kirk decided to take his time getting back to the bridge. The turbolift could get him there in seconds, but he wanted to walk her decks.

On the way, he saw Miranda Tikolo and Stanley Vandella, deep in conversation. As he grew closer, the conversation ended with a surprisingly chaste hug. Vandella nodded to Kirk and disappeared down the corridor, and Tikolo waited for him to reach her.

"Are you two . . . ?" he began.

"Oh, no. No, I'm afraid that's over," she said. "I couldn't possibly be any good to anybody in a romantic way. Not right now. Not after . . . everything."

The captain wondered if she meant Paul O'Meara's death, which McCoy had told Tikolo about once she was safely on board the *Enterprise* and fully recovered from the stun. She was a young lady with a very strong personality.

"That might be for the best." He moved to walk away, but she stopped him.

"Sir," she said, "I was just about to go looking for you."

Kirk turned toward her again. "Here I am."

"I . . . I need to resign my commission," Tikolo said. "I am so grateful that you offered me a position on your ship. I was made to feel welcomed . . . and worthwhile. But obviously I'm just not ready. I need to work through a lot of issues."

"You can't do that aboard the *Enterprise*?"

"No, sir. I mean, I don't ever want to be a danger to anybody again. Until I can trust myself, I can't ask anyone else to trust me."

"If that's what you want," Kirk said.

"It is, sir. You see, Nurse Chapel told me something about myself I didn't even know. It's . . . it's pretty horrible. But at the same time, it helps explain a lot. I'm not saying that I'm not responsible for my own decisions, my own actions. I am. But given what I've been through, it's possible that I didn't have a lot of choice in the matter, either. The decisions I make are determined by the person that I am, and that person is, in a lot of ways, a mess."

Kirk nodded. He had been briefed on Tikolo's childhood trauma, and he was sure it had come as a shock to her. "When you are ready," he said, "come back. You'll always have a berth here."

"Thank you, Captain."

"You're a fine officer, and you'll be a better one. I'd rather have you on my crew than hear about your exploits on behalf of some other starship."

"I will request your ship," she said. "Definitely."

"Good," he said. "Whenever you're ready. There's plenty of space yet to be explored, and the *Enterprise* will be here for you. In the meantime . . ."

"Yes, sir?"

"If you're looking for a therapeutic activity, I can make a recommendation."

She pressed her hands together in front of her chest. "Really?" Tikolo asked. "What is it?"

"Back on Earth, in rural Idaho," he began, "there are these cattle drives . . ."

Acknowledgments

Writing is a solitary profession, but somehow by the time a novel is finished there are many hands involved, whether they know it or not. Some of those who helped make this one a reality are editors Margaret Clark and Ed Schlesinger, my agent Howard Morhaim and his assistant, Alice Speilburg. For inspiration and information I look to the warm and welcoming community of *Star Trek* writers, editors, and fans present and past, who let me through the door again (including, but by no means limited to, Greg Cox, Keith DeCandido, John Ordover, David George, Dayton Ward, Geoffrey Thorne, Marco Palmieri, Kevin Dilmore, and so many more). Marcy Rockwell helped keep me (arguably) sane as I worked on it during a difficult summer. Dianne Larson kept my website sane. And as always, Maryelizabeth Hart, Holly Mariotte, and David Mariotte remain the foundation of everything. Thanks to all of you.

About the Author

Jeff Mariotte is the author of more than forty-five novels, including the supernatural thrillers *Season of the Wolf, River Runs Red, Missing White Girl,* and *Cold Black Hearts,* the thriller *The Devil's Bait,* the horror epic *The Slab,* the *Dark Vengeance* teen horror quartet, and others, as well as dozens of comic books, notably *Desperadoes* and *Zombie Cop.* He has written books, stories, and comics set in beloved fictional universes, including those of *Buffy the Vampire Slayer* and *Angel, CSI* and *CSI: Miami, The Shield, Criminal Minds, Conan, Superman, Spider-Man, Hellraiser,* and many more, and is a two-time winner of the Scribe Award presented by the International Association of Media Tie-in Writers. He's a co-owner of the specialty bookstore Mysterious Galaxy in San Diego, and lives in southeastern Arizona on the Flying M Ranch. Please visit him at www.jeffmariotte.com or http://www.facebook.com/JeffreyJMariotte.